The Sleepover Club

Have you been invited to all these sleepovers?

1. The Sleepover Club at Frankie's
2. The Sleepover Club at Lyndsey's
3. The Sleepover Club at Felicity's
4. The Sleepover Club at Rosie's
5. The Sleepover Club at Laura's
6. Starring the Sleepover Club
7. Sleepover Girls go Pop!
8. The 24-Hour Sleepover Club
9. The Sleepover Club Sleeps Out
10. Happy Birthday Sleepover Club
11. Sleepover Girls on Horseback
12. Sleepover in Spain
13. Sleepover on Friday 13th
14. Sleepover Girls go Camping
15. Sleepover Girls go Detective
16. Sleepover Girls go Designer
17. The Sleepover Club Surfs the Net
18. Sleepover Girls on Screen
19. Sleepover Girls and Friends
20. Sleepover Girls on the Catwalk
21. The Sleepover Club Goes for Goal!
22. Sleepover Girls go Babysitting
23. Sleepover Girls go Snowboarding
24. Happy New Year, Sleepover Club!
25. Sleepover Girls go Green
26. We Love You Sleepover Club
27. Vive le Sleepover Club!
28. Sleepover Club Eggstravaganza
29. Emergency Sleepover
30. Sleepover Girls on the Range
31. The Sleepover Club Bridesmaids
32. Sleepover Girls See Stars
33. Sleepover Club Blitz
34. Sleepover Girls in the Ring
35. Sari Sleepover
36. Merry Christmas Sleepover Club!
37. The Sleepover Club Down Under
38. Sleepover Girls go Splash!
39. Sleepover Girls go Karting
40. Sleepover Girls go Wild!
41. The Sleepover Club at the Carnival
42. The Sleepover Club on the Beach
43. Sleepover Club Vampires
44. sleepoverclub.com
45. Sleepover Girls go Dancing
46. The Sleepover Club on the Farm
47. Sleepover Girls go Gymtastic!

Sleepover Girls on the Ball

by Narinder Dhami

Collins
An imprint of HarperCollins*Publishers*

The Sleepover Club ® is a
registered trademark of HarperCollins*Publishers* Ltd

First published in Great Britain by Collins in 2001
Collins is an imprint of HarperCollins*Publishers* Ltd
77-85 Fulham Palace Road, Hammersmith,
London, W6 8JB

The HarperCollins website address is
www.**fire**and**water**.com

1 3 5 7 9 8 6 4 2

Text copyright © Narinder Dhami 2002

Original series characters, plotlines
and settings © Rose Impey 1997

ISBN 0-00-713290-5

The author asserts the moral right to
be identified as the author of the work.

Printed in Great Britain by
Clays Ltd, St Ives plc

Conditions of Sale
This book is sold subject to the condition
that it shall not, by way of trade or otherwise,
be lent, re-sold, hired out or otherwise circulated
without the publisher's prior consent in any form,
binding or cover other than that in which it is
published and without a similar condition
including this condition being imposed
on the subsequent purchaser.

Sleepover Kit List

1. Sleeping bag
2. Pillow
3. Pyjamas or a nightdress
4. Slippers
5. Toothbrush, toothpaste, soap etc
6. Towel
7. Teddy
8. A creepy story
9. Food for a midnight feast: chocolate, crisps, sweets, biscuits. In fact anything you like to eat.
10. Torch
11. Hairbrush
12. Hair things like a bobble or hairband, if you need them
13. Clean knickers and socks
14. Change of clothes for the next day
15. Sleepover diary and membership card

CHAPTER ONE

"Well, I think we should do something *really* cool and totally exciting," said Kenny. "Something we've never done before, like hang-gliding. Or parachute jumps. Or mountain-climbing."

We all fell about laughing. That's Kenny for you. She's totally mad. But you know that, don't you? Or maybe you don't! And if you don't, where have you been all this time? Haven't you *heard* of the Sleepover Club?

"There aren't any mountains in Cuddington," I pointed out. Cuddington's the village where we all live. (What do you mean – who are we? Keep reading, and you'll find out!)

"I wouldn't jump out of an aeroplane," Rosie

The Sleepover Club

said with a shudder. She took a drink of Coke, and put the can down on the grass. Kenny winked at me, and quickly dropped something into the open triangle on the top of the can. Rosie and Lyndz didn't notice. "What if your parachute didn't open?"

"*Ker-splatttt!*" Kenny said. "That's what!"

"I don't like heights," Lyndz said. She opened a bag of prawn cocktail crisps and offered it round. "Anyway, I'd rather go riding."

"Oh, you lot are so *boring*!" Kenny moaned. "Look, we've got six whole weeks of holidays, and we've got to decide what we're going to do. Any ideas?"

We all thought for a bit. It was the last day of term, and we were sitting in the playground after lunch. In a few hours, we'd be free for the whole summer.

"We can have lots of sleepovers," Lyndz suggested.

OK, so now you know why we're called the Sleepover Club. Frankie, Kenny, Lyndz, Rosie and Fliss – that's us.

"Yeah, we can talk about the holidays at the sleepover at Fliss's place tonight," I said.

"Where *is* Fliss, anyway?" Kenny asked.

"She said she had some books to return to the school library," I replied. "She should be here in a minute."

"Oh, well, she'll only want to do *girly* things," Kenny said, pulling a gruesome face.

"There's loads of stuff on the school noticeboard," Lyndz said, "all about summer camps and courses. There's things going on at the local library too."

"Maybe we should take a look," Rosie said, having another drink. She tipped up the can to finish it, then frowned. "Hey, there's something in here!"

"What?" Lyndz asked.

Rosie spat it out into her hand. "Urgh!" she yelled in disgust. "It's a fingernail!"

"Is it one of yours?" Kenny asked, keeping a perfectly straight face. Meanwhile, Lyndz and I were in hysterics.

"No, why would I put a fingernail in my can of Coke?" Rosie screeched. Then she took a closer look. "Hang on, this is plastic!"

"Oh, sorry," Kenny said innocently. "Did you want a real one?"

Rosie burst out laughing. "I'm going to kill you, Laura McKenzie!" she said between giggles.

"Let's all help," I said. "Get her!"

Kenny gave a yell as Rosie, Lyndz and I piled on top of her.

"No more jokes for the whole summer, Kenny!" I ordered her. "Is that a deal?"

"No way!" Kenny groaned. "If the summer's going to be dead boring, I'm definitely going to carry on playing jokes."

"There must be *something* we can do," I said, as we all rolled off her. "What kind of things were on the noticeboard, Lyndz?"

"There's a Book Week at the library," Lyndz replied. "And a nature trail walk, and a visit to the local museum."

"Cool," Kenny said sarcastically. "I think I'm going to pass out with all the excitement!"

"Anything else?" Rosie asked.

"There's a week's tennis coaching at the local college," Lyndz added.

"Tennis!" Kenny said in disgust. "I hate tennis. It's so *boring*."

We were a bit surprised. There's not many sports Kenny *doesn't* like.

"It's so dull," Kenny moaned. "All they do is hit a ball over a net."

"Well, all footballers do is try to *kick* a ball

Sleepover Girls on the Ball

into a net!" I pointed out. Kenny's football-mad. But I knew what she meant. I wasn't that keen on tennis either.

"And then it starts to rain, and everyone rushes inside like a bunch of wimps," Kenny went on. "Footballers don't do that."

"Yeah, and what's with those scores?" Rosie said. "I mean, fifteen, thirty, forty. It doesn't make sense."

"Then there's all that love-this and love-that, too," Lyndz chimed in. "And what's that juice bit all about?"

"You mean deuce," Kenny, Rosie and I said together.

"Oh." Lyndz turned pink. "I thought it meant they were thirsty!"

We got the giggles then.

"You know what I hate," Rosie said, when we'd calmed down a bit. "The way all the other TV programmes are taken off when Wimbledon's on."

"Oh, yeah," I agreed. "We don't get to see *Neighbours* for two whole weeks. How mean is that?"

"My mum's mad on tennis," Lyndz said. "She watches it all day, when it's on."

The Sleepover Club

"Mine too," I agreed.

"So does our Tiff," Rosie added.

"So does Molly the Monster," Kenny said gloomily. That's her sister, by the way.

"OK, so none of us like tennis," I said. "Let's forget about it, and decide what we *want* to do."

"I can't wait for next week," said a snooty voice just behind us. "I'm really looking forward to the tennis coaching. Aren't you, Emily?"

We knew who it was, of course. There's only one person in the whole world who's that snotty. Our arch-enemy, Emma Hughes, and her weedy little sidekick, Emily Berryman, also known as the M&Ms – or the Queen and the Goblin.

"And we'll be able to practise at the Green Lawns club," Emily said in her gruff, goblin-like voice. "I'm really glad we've joined."

"Yes, it's one of the best tennis clubs in England, you know," the Queen said. She is *such* a big fat snob. "And don't forget they're having that special gala afternoon next week to celebrate the club being open for fifty years. That'll be fun."

Sleepover Girls on the Ball

OK, so we were listening. We couldn't help it. It was *so* typical of the M&Ms to go around boasting at the top of their voices.

Emma Hughes spotted us earwigging. She put this face on like she'd just swallowed a whole lemon.

"Haven't you lot got anything better to do than listen to other people's conversations?" she snapped.

"No," Kenny said.

That floored the Queen.

"Well, just mind your own business," she said feebly.

Kenny shrugged. "I might've known those two wimps would be into tennis," she said, loud enough for Emma and Emily to hear.

Emma glared at us. "And I might've known you idiots *wouldn't* be," she retorted.

"What's that supposed to mean?" I asked.

The Queen and the Goblin smirked. "You lot wouldn't be allowed into Green Lawns," Emma Hughes sniffed snootily. "Tennis is a game for *nice* people who've got lots of money."

"Are you saying we're not posh enough for your stupid club?" Kenny was getting quite annoyed now. I glanced at Lyndz and Rosie.

The Sleepover Club

We might just have to sit on her again to stop her jumping on Emma!

"That's right," Emily said gruffly.

The Queen and the Goblin looked very pleased with themselves, because they thought they'd got one over on us. They soon stopped though, when Kenny took a step towards them.

"I wouldn't want to be in any club that you two were members of, anyway!" Kenny snorted. "And tennis is a load of rubbish. You wouldn't catch me playing a daft game like that."

"Yeah, tennis is for wimps like you who are too scared to play proper games," I joined in.

"So don't worry," Rosie added, "we wouldn't be seen dead at your stupid tennis club."

"Now push off and stop bothering us," Lyndz finished up.

"Take no notice of them, Emma," the Goblin muttered as they walked off with their noses in the air. "They're just jealous."

"I know," the Queen agreed. "Wait till you see my two-handed backhand, Emily. It's my best shot." She swung out with an imaginary tennis racket, and hit the Goblin smack on the shoulder.

"Ow!" Emily yowled. Which had us all in fits, of course.

"Those two have got a nerve," Kenny grumbled. She grabbed Lyndz's empty crisp packet, blew it up and then burst it with a loud bang. "Fancy telling us we're not posh enough to join their tennis club."

"Yeah, fancy that!" I grinned.

"Well, now that we're *definitely* not going to play tennis over the summer, what are we going to do?" Rosie asked.

"Here's Fliss," Lyndz said.

Fliss came hurrying across the playground towards us. She was looking pretty pleased with herself.

"Hiya, Flissy." Kenny waved at her. "We're just talking about what we're going to do over the holidays."

"Yeah, have you got any suggestions?" I asked.

"But not too girly," Kenny added.

"We can't think of anything much," Lyndz said.

Fliss grinned at us.

The Sleepover Club

"It's all sorted," she said. "Well, the first week of the holidays is, anyway. It's going to be really excellent!"

We all sat up, looking interested.

"So what are we going to be doing?" Rosie asked eagerly.

Fliss beamed at us. "I've signed us all up for a week's tennis coaching at the local college!"

CHAPTER TWO

We were all too stunned to say anything for a moment. Then Kenny jumped to her feet.

"You've done *what*?" she roared.

"I knew you'd be pleased," Fliss said chirpily. "We get a whole week of coaching, and..." Her voice tailed off as she looked round at us. "What's the matter?"

"We all hate tennis, that's what's the matter!" I pointed out. "Fliss, why didn't you ask us first?"

Fliss turned pink. "I thought you'd be pleased," she mumbled.

"We've just told the M&Ms that we wouldn't be seen dead playing tennis!" Kenny groaned.

The Sleepover Club

"They're going to laugh their heads off if we turn up for those coaching sessions now."

"Fliss, you're going to have to cross our names off that list," Rosie said.

"But I *like* tennis," Fliss said stubbornly. "Come on, it'll be a laugh. And the guy who's doing the coaching is really nice."

"How do you know?" Lyndz asked.

"I – er – just heard that he was," Fliss replied, blushing madly.

I glanced at Rosie, Lyndz and Kenny. They looked about as impressed as I was. None of us wanted to spend one whole week of our precious holiday doing something we didn't like and just weren't interested in. Then, all of a sudden, I remembered something.

"Hold on a minute, Fliss," I said slowly. "Has this got something to do with your Auntie Jill?"

"No," Fliss said, trying not to look guilty. "Why?"

"Because I remember you saying that your Auntie Jill was going out with a tennis coach." I stared hard at Fliss, and she began to fidget. She was always *hopeless* at telling fibs!

"Oh, all right." Fliss gave in. "Auntie Jill's boyfriend, Mark, is the one who's running the course. And she asked me to get as many people signed up as I could."

"Oh, great," Kenny grumbled. "Why does it have to be *us*?"

"Look, it's only for a week," Fliss pleaded. "And you like my Auntie Jill, don't you? She'd be really grateful."

That kind of made it difficult for us. We *did* like Fliss's Auntie Jill. She was our Snowy Owl at Brownies, and she was a great laugh.

"If you all come, I'll do whatever you want for the rest of the summer," Fliss promised.

"What, anything?" Kenny said with an evil grin.

"Anything," Fliss said bravely.

"OK, I'm in," Kenny sighed, rolling her eyes. "I must be crazy."

Rosie and Lyndz nodded. So did I.

"Oh, great!" Fliss gasped. She was really pleased, but the rest of us looked like we'd agreed to spend a week at the dentist having our teeth pulled out one by one.

Still, it was only for a week. It couldn't be that bad.

Could it?

* * *

The Sleepover Club

"Tennis?"

My mum stared at me as if I'd said we planned to spend a week of the summer holidays learning Chinese. "You girls are going to play *tennis*?"

I nodded. "What's so strange about that?"

"Well, for one thing, you moan like mad every time I watch Wimbledon," my mum pointed out, bouncing my baby sister Izzy on her hip. "You said you hated tennis."

"Long story, Mum." I picked up my sleepover bag. School had finished – at last! – and I was in my bedroom, packing for the sleepover at Fliss's. "Anyway, that's what we're doing."

"Oh, well, I suppose it'll keep you out of trouble," my mum said. Then she shook her head. "Why on earth did I say that? *Nothing* keeps you girls out of trouble."

"Thanks a lot, Mum," I grumbled, stuffing my purple pyjamas into my bag. "We're only going to be messing around with rackets and tennis balls, you know. What could *possibly* go wrong?"

"Quite a lot, with Kenny around," my mum replied.

The doorbell rang.

Sleepover Girls on the Ball

"That'll be Rosie," I said, grabbing my bag. Rosie's mum had arranged to pick us all up and take us round to Fliss's. "'Bye, Mum, 'bye, Izzy."

Rosie was waiting for me on the doorstep, and Kenny and Lyndz were in the car with Mrs Cartwright. I squeezed into the back seat next to them.

"So you're all going to be playing tennis next week," Mrs Cartwright remarked, as she drove off. Like my mum, she seemed to think that this was somehow really funny. Parents! You wouldn't have them if they were being given away, would you? "I hope you're going to behave yourselves."

"Mum!" Rosie muttered, looking embarrassed.

"'Course we will, Mrs Cartwright," Kenny said in that voice which meant she was up to something. I glanced sideways at her. She winked at me.

"Tell you later," she hissed.

Mrs Cartwright dropped us off at Fliss's house, and we all trooped up to the front door.

"Flissy really owes us one for this," Kenny grumbled, ringing the doorbell and keeping her finger on it. "I can't believe what she's got us into."

"It might be OK," Lyndz said hopefully.

"Maybe we could all pretend to injure ourselves on the first day," Rosie suggested. "Fliss couldn't expect us to play if we were in agony."

"Want to bet?" Kenny muttered. "Anyway, don't you think it might look a bit obvious if we *all* sprain our ankles? Oh come on, Fliss!" she added, leaning extra hard on the doorbell.

Fliss opened the door with her hands over her ears.

"Kenny, what're you doing!" she said crossly.

We stared at her. Fliss was wearing a short white dress, and I mean *short*. Fliss loves miniskirts, but this was ridiculous. It was right up round the tops of her legs.

"Aren't you a bit cold?" Kenny asked, as we all went inside.

"This is my new tennis dress." Fliss did a twirl in the hallway. "Do you like it?"

"It's a bit short," Lyndz said.

"Yeah, we can see your knickers," Kenny added.

"You're supposed to see them," Fliss snapped.

"Why?" Rosie asked.

Sleepover Girls on the Ball

"Well, because tennis dresses are always short," Fliss said feebly.

"Why?" Lyndz wanted to know.

Fliss looked blank.

"So you can run around in them easily, I suppose," I suggested.

"Yeah, that's right," Fliss agreed quickly. "Come on, I've got some really great ideas for the sleepover tonight."

We all looked interested.

"I thought we'd have a tennis sleepover," Fliss said eagerly. "We can play tennis in the garden, and Mum's got some strawberries and cream for tea just like they have at Wimbledon. Oh, and I've got some tennis videos we can watch afterwards."

"You're kidding!" Kenny began indignantly, "That sounds like a load of— OW!"

I took my foot off her big toe.

"That sounds great, Fliss," I said.

"Yeah, great," said Rosie and Lyndz glumly.

Fliss looked pleased. "Come on, let's go into the back garden," she said.

We followed her into the kitchen. Fliss's mum and her mum's sister, Auntie Jill, were sitting at the breakfast bar, having coffee.

"Oh, hello, girls." Auntie Jill grinned at us. "I hear you're going to Mark's coaching sessions next week."

We nodded.

"I didn't know you girls were interested in tennis," Mrs Proudlove said, taking a sip of coffee.

We all started shuffling our feet and looking a bit sheepish.

"Come on," Fliss said hastily. "Let's go outside."

"Jill and I had a game today," Mrs Proudlove went on. "It was pretty close, wasn't it, Jill? I won, though!"

"That was a great overhead lob you pulled off at match point," Auntie Jill said. "It had a lot of topspin on it."

"And what about that forehand drive you won the second game with?" Fliss's mum added. "The way you smashed that down the line was brilliant."

I glanced at Kenny, who rolled her eyes at me. Mrs Proudlove and Auntie Jill might as well have been talking Greek for all we could understand! Were we the only people in the world who weren't tennis-mad?

Sleepover Girls on the Ball

"Oh, Mum, have you heard anything from the Green Lawns Tennis Club yet?" Fliss asked, as she opened the back door.

Kenny nudged me. That was the same club the M&Ms belonged to.

Mrs Proudlove shook her head. "Not yet," she said. "Your auntie and I played on the tennis courts in the park today. We're still waiting to hear if we can join the club."

"Well, Mark's put in a good word for us," Auntie Jill said. She turned to us and added, "Mark works at Green Lawns. It's one of the best tennis clubs in the country, you know."

"You didn't tell us your mum and Auntie Jill wanted to join that snooty club," Kenny accused Fliss, as we went outside.

"It's not snooty," Fliss said indignantly.

"Well, the M&Ms go there, so it must be," I pointed out.

Fliss pouted. "I don't care," she said. "If Mum and Auntie Jill get in, they can take guests, so I'll be able to play there too."

"Do you reckon Fliss is really keen on tennis?" Kenny whispered in my ear.

"I reckon she just likes the short skirts!" I whispered back.

The Sleepover Club

Fliss was bustling about giving out rackets and tennis balls.

"I've got my own racket," she said importantly, waving it in the air. "You can have this one, Rosie."

Rosie stared at the racket she'd just been given. It was about a hundred years old, and half the strings were broken.

"Sorry," Fliss said. "It's my mum's old one."

"Can't I borrow her new one?" Rosie asked.

Fliss shook her head. "It cost loads of money. She said I could only borrow it over her dead body."

"What about the rest of us?" Kenny asked.

"I've only got two rackets," Fliss said apologetically. "We'll have to take it in turns."

Kenny didn't look very impressed.

"Can't we play something else?" she grumbled.

"We're playing *tennis*." Fliss glared at Kenny. "Now go and sit down. You lot can watch while me and Rosie go first."

"Big deal," Kenny moaned under her breath, as we all sat down on the grass. "This is so boring!"

"Ssh!" I nudged her. "It's Fliss's sleepover, and you know what she's like."

Kenny yawned. "If I die from boredom, you can have my pet rat!"

"Thanks a lot," I said, as Fliss threw the ball into the air, and hit it towards Rosie.

Rosie stepped forward, looking a bit nervous. I thought she'd miss the ball, but she didn't. She gave it a THWACK. At least, she tried to. When the ball hit her racket, there was a snapping sound as it smashed through the dodgy strings, and out the other side. We all watched open-mouthed as the ball sailed over the fence, and into the Watson-Wades' garden next door. Then there was a SPLASH as it fell into their pond.

We all started to laugh our heads off, except Fliss, who turned pale. The Watson-Wades don't like us, and we don't like them either. We call them the Grumpies.

"Quick, into the house!" she hissed, and we all dashed inside. Kenny could hardly walk, she was laughing so much.

"No more tennis!" she whispered gleefully in my ear. "Maybe we can do something more exciting now instead."

"OK, let's watch some of my tennis videos," Fliss said. She was on her knees in front of the TV, sorting through them.

I thought Kenny was going to kill her, but luckily Mrs Proudlove called to say tea was ready.

Tea was pretty boring, too. The food was OK, but Mrs Proudlove, Auntie Jill and Fliss just went on about tennis for the whole meal. They were talking about forehands and backhands and lobs and volleys until our heads were spinning like tennis balls!

We couldn't escape from tennis after tea, either. Fliss put one of her videos on, and we sat and watched them until we went to bed. Kenny fell asleep and started snoring, which really annoyed Fliss.

"That has to be the most mega-boring sleepover of all time," Kenny moaned under her breath, as we trailed upstairs to Fliss's bedroom at the end of the evening.

"Last one in the bathroom is useless at tennis!" Fliss yelled, grabbing her pink pyjamas. She dashed off down the landing, while the rest of us looked gloomily at each other.

"I don't care about being last," Rosie said.

"Me neither," Kenny added. And she's usually the one who pushes us all out of the way!

Lyndz looked round at us. "Maybe we *could* get to like tennis," she suggested.

Kenny chucked a pillow at her.

"No, really," Lyndz went on. "Anyway, even if we don't like it, we can still have a laugh at the coaching sessions. We've got to go to them now, so there's no point in moaning about it."

Kenny grinned an evil grin. "Yeah, Lyndz is right," she said. "Remember I said I'd got something to tell you, Frankie?"

I nodded.

"Well, the M&Ms are going to the tennis coaching too, aren't they?" Kenny went on. "And they take tennis ever so seriously. That means…"

"A chance to play a whole load of jokes on them," I finished up.

Kenny rubbed her hands together with glee. "Yep! Tennis might be boring, but the Sleepover Club will soon liven it up!"

CHAPTER THREE

"I'm sure you're going to have a great time, girls," Auntie Jill said, as she turned into the college driveway. "Mark's a fantastic coach. He'll soon have you all playing like professionals!"

It was the first day of our week of tennis coaching at the local college. Auntie Jill had borrowed the Proudloves' people carrier, and had arranged to drive us to the college.

"So that none of us can make a break for it and escape!" Kenny had moaned to me. Still, we *had* all decided that we would make the best of things, and it *was* only for a week.

Kenny nudged me as we drove through the

college grounds, then drew up outside the tennis courts.

"Hey, everyone," she said with a grin. "Don't look now, or you might bring up your breakfast!"

We all looked out of the window. Not many people had arrived yet, but guess who was there already, swanning round the tennis courts as if they owned them? The Queen and the Goblin, of course. Emma Hughes was wearing a white lacy tennis dress which was shorter than Fliss's, if that was possible! And Emily Berryman was wearing this really tight pair of white shorts that looked truly gruesome.

"They really think they're something, don't they?" Kenny said scornfully, as we climbed out of the people carrier. "I'm looking forward to annoying them!"

The M&Ms were carrying rackets that looked really posh. I don't know anything about tennis rackets, but these were definitely pretty flash. None of us had our own racket except Fliss, and we were all wearing different sorts of clothes. Fliss had her white tennis dress on (of course!), and Rosie, Lyndz and I were wearing trackie bottoms and T-shirts in various colours. Kenny had decided

The Sleepover Club

to put her Leicester City football strip on, for some reason.

Just then the M&Ms spotted us walking towards the tennis courts. The Queen's eyes almost fell out of her head, and she and the Goblin started nudging each other. They had these big fat smirks on their faces too.

"I'll go and see if I can find Mark," Auntie Jill said, and headed off towards the changing-rooms.

"Funny," the Queen said in this really loud, incredibly smug voice that we were obviously meant to hear. "I thought tennis was for *wimps*."

"Yeah, for people who are too *scared* to play proper games," the Goblin chimed in gruffly. Then they both laughed their heads off as if they'd just said something really funny.

"It is," Kenny retorted breezily. "We're just here to help Mark out."

The Queen and the Goblin stopped laughing.

"Mark?" Emma Hughes spluttered. "You don't know Mark!"

"We do, though," Berryman added. "He's one of the coaches at Green Lawns."

"Yes, well, he goes out with my Auntie Jill," Fliss said, looking pretty smug herself.

Sleepover Girls on the Ball

The M&Ms glared at her in disbelief – and right at that moment Auntie Jill came out of the changing-rooms with this hunky guy behind her. He looked a bit like Robbie Williams, and he was *gorgeous*!

"Hi, Fliss," he said with a smile. "And these must be your friends. Nice to see you all." He looked at the M&Ms. "Hi, I'm Mark, the tennis coach. And you are?"

The Queen looked a bit annoyed.

"Emma Hughes and Emily Berryman," she reminded him. "We go to Green Lawns."

"Oh, yes, sorry," Mark said. "I'd forgotten."

We all tried not to snigger.

"I'll see you later," Auntie Jill said, and then she left. Meanwhile, Mark took a list from his pocket and ticked our names off.

"I'll just go and check the others off my list," he said. "And then we'll get started."

More and more people were arriving, including Ryan Scott and Danny McCloud, two real idiots who're in our class. Fliss started blushing, and fluttering her eyelashes, though. She's totally in love with Ryan, but she tries to pretend she isn't!

The Queen and the Goblin trotted after

Mark, being real creeps and asking lots of questions. Kenny pulled a face at them, and flopped down on a nearby bench.

"Those two are going to drive me bananas!" she groaned. "Hello, what's this?"

There were two big *Nike* sports bags, by the side of the bench.

"Those are the Queen's and the Goblin's," Rosie said. "I've seen them at school."

"Oh, really," Kenny said with an evil smile. She bounced off the bench, and bent over one of the bags.

"Kenny, what are you doing?" Fliss hissed, in a total panic. "You can't open their bags. If Mark sees us, we're dead!"

"Relax, Flissy," Kenny said. "I wouldn't dream of opening someone else's bag."

Fliss looked relieved. "Oh, good."

"This one's already open," Kenny went on. "Look, it's the Queen's." She pointed at the name written on the handle, then she put her hand into the bag and pulled out a pair of expensive-looking trainers. "Phew, these really stink!"

"Trust the Queen and the Goblin to have special trainers for tennis," I said.

Fliss turned pink. "Actually," she said, clearing her throat, "so do I!"

"Quick," Kenny said urgently. "Stand a bit closer so that no one can see me for a minute."

We all gathered round Kenny and hid her from view. By the time Mark and the others, including the M&Ms, came over, we were all sitting innocently on the bench, and the trainers were back in the Queen's bag.

"Right, welcome to our summer tennis school," Mark said briskly. "A week isn't really very long, but hopefully I'll be able to give you some good advice to improve your game. And if you're a beginner, well, maybe you'll find out if you're any good or not. And maybe you'll find you like tennis a lot more than you thought you would!"

Kenny rolled her eyes at the rest of us. "No chance!" she whispered.

"Now, if you could just divide yourselves into groups of four," Mark went on, "we'll start off with a bit of a knock-up, and I'll come round and see how you're all getting on."

Everyone moved off in groups, and began to spread out around the courts.

"What about us?" Lyndz asked anxiously. "There's five of us."

"It's OK," I said, doing a quick headcount. "There's seventeen people here, so there'll have to be one group of five."

"Come on, Emily." The Queen pushed rudely past us with her nose in the air. "Let's change into our other trainers."

"Here we go!" Kenny whispered with a big grin.

"Oh no." The Queen's face dropped as she pulled her trainers out of her bag. "They're all knotted up!"

We turned our backs, trying not to laugh. Kenny had tied the laces together with about a million knots!

"It's going to take you ages to undo them," the Goblin grumbled.

We left them to it, grabbed some rackets and balls and ran off to bag a court. We were right next to Ryan Scott and Danny McCloud, who were already belting balls around as if they were playing cricket.

"You're supposed to keep it inside the white lines," Rosie shouted at them, as Ryan whacked yet another ball way over Danny's head. Then we all jumped smartly out of the way as Danny mis-hit the next one, and it came thundering towards us.

"Trust us to be next to those two," Kenny grumbled, as we split up into two teams. Rosie and Fliss were on one side of the net, and Kenny, Lyndz and I were on the other. "They're going to do us an injury at this rate!"

Fliss threw a ball into the air, served and smacked it down to Kenny. I don't think Kenny was expecting Fliss to hit it quite so hard. She stuck out her racket, and the ball bounced off the frame instead of the strings. It flew off to the side at an angle, and almost took Danny McCloud's ear off.

"Hey!" Danny shouted indignantly. "Trust us to get landed next to those mad girls," we heard him say to Ryan.

Fliss changed sides, and served to Lyndz this time. She hit the ball hard again, and Lyndz gave a little yelp and jumped right out of the way. She didn't even try to hit it.

"Lyndz, you do know what tennis is all about, don't you?" I said. "You have to try and return the ball."

"I know," Lyndz said gloomily, "But that was scary! Fliss hit the ball too hard."

"Fliss is just showing off," Kenny said to me and Lyndz in a low voice. "Let us serve this time," she called across the net to the others. "Go on, Frankie."

"OK," I agreed. I'd never done it before, but if Fliss could do it, how hard could it be?

I threw the ball up into the air, and then raised my arm above my head to smash it.

"Hey, was that an ace?" I yelled proudly, as Fliss and Rosie stood staring at me. "The ball moved so fast, I didn't even see it."

"Frankie, I think there's something you should know," Kenny said, pointing at my feet. I looked down. There was the ball.

"You missed it," Lyndz said helpfully.

I blushed. I grabbed the ball, bounced it on the ground and just knocked it over the net. Rosie raced towards it, elbowing Fliss out of the way, and hit the ball with all her might. It soared right over the high fence that surrounded the tennis courts, and bounced into some bushes.

"Hey, you're supposed to keep the ball *inside* the courts!" Ryan Scott shouted, and he and Danny laughed themselves silly.

Sleepover Girls on the Ball

"Come on," Kenny said impatiently, "I'm getting bored with this. I want to try out my trick shots."

"What trick shots?" Fliss asked suspiciously, as Rosie tapped another ball over the net to Kenny. It was a lot lower and slower this time. Kenny immediately ran round the ball so that she had her back to the net. Then she scooped it up and flipped it over her head. It dropped gently over the net, and then rolled away from Fliss, who was running towards it.

"Kenny, that's not a proper shot!" Fliss said disapprovingly.

"What a load of rubbish," the Queen sniffed. She and the Goblin had come over, and had stopped to watch what we were doing. "Some people will *never* be good at tennis."

"We've got to play with you," Emily Berryman said to Ryan and Danny. "There aren't any more courts left."

We saw Ryan and Danny pull faces at each other.

"OK, but don't try to boss us around," Ryan said shortly.

The Queen and the Goblin started playing against each other, on the side of the court closest to us. Kenny was still messing around and having a go at all sorts of tricks, like trying to catch the ball on her racket instead of hitting it back, and trying to hit the ball between her legs. It was driving Fliss crazy.

Anyway, I couldn't help watching the M&Ms. To my surprise, they were pretty good. They aren't exactly sporty types, but they looked all right at tennis. The other thing that surprised me was that Fliss was good too. Whenever she managed to get the ball, she always did something I was *sure* I wouldn't be able to do myself.

While Rosie and Fliss were collecting up the balls we'd hit all over the place, I nudged Kenny. "Have you seen the M&Ms? They're not bad at this."

"What?" Kenny's eyes almost popped out of her head. She watched the Queen and the Goblin for a few moments, and then nodded reluctantly. "Yeah, I suppose they're OK. Sick-making, isn't it?"

"Fliss is good too, isn't she?" Lyndz added.

"Hmm." Kenny was frowning. I knew exactly what was going through her mind. "Come on, let's start practising. We don't want the M&Ms getting one over on us."

"But I thought we were here to have a laugh?" Lyndz said.

"Never mind that," Kenny ordered us. "We'd better start taking this a bit more seriously."

Just then Mark came over to us. He'd been walking round the courts, watching everyone and talking to them, and now it was our turn.

"Over here, girls," he said, beckoning us over to the net. "How are you getting on?"

"Fine," Fliss mumbled, glaring at Kenny. I felt a bit sorry for her. She was way better than the rest of us, and she was fed up with Kenny and the rest of us messing around when she wanted to have a proper game.

"Good." Mark nodded. "Now, I've been watching you for the last few minutes, and I think you've got the makings of a very good forehand drive there, Kenny."

Kenny looked amazed. "R-really?" she stuttered.

Mark grinned. "Yes, but I don't think the trick shots are helping, so cut them out, OK? And Frankie – we'll be working on our serves later, so don't worry about that."

The Sleepover Club

I turned red.

"Carry on knocking up for another few minutes," Mark said, glancing at his watch. "And then we'll all get together for some practice shots."

"Come on, you lot," Kenny shouted, herding us back on to the court. "And *concentrate* this time!"

Fliss looked smug. "See?" she said. "I told you you'd enjoy it!"

And we *were* starting to enjoy it. Once we stopped messing about, and began trying harder, we got better. Fliss showed us some of her shots, and we tried to copy her. We weren't very good, but at least we were better than before. She also showed us how to serve, and this time I actually managed to hit the ball!

Then Mark called us all together, and began talking to us about different types of shots.

"We're going to start with a simple forehand," he said, and then he told us how important it was to hold the racket properly, and have the right grip. We all had to practise holding our rackets, and swinging them at an imaginary ball. There was so much to remember, I couldn't take it all in. It wasn't just about how you hit the ball

– you also had to follow through properly, and end up with the racket in a certain place *after* you'd hit the ball. Confused? I was!

"Right, line up behind the net," Mark called. "I want you to step forward one by one, and hit the ball back to me with your forehand. Remember what we've just been talking about, and try to follow through correctly. Fliss, you first."

Mark hit the ball over the net to Fliss, and she hit it back. It looked pretty good to me. Then Kenny stepped up.

"Just watch her make a mess of this!" we heard the Queen whisper to the Goblin.

Kenny didn't say anything. She whacked the ball, and it whizzed neatly just over the net and bounced into one corner of the court.

"Excellent, Kenny!" Mark called, and the Queen and the Goblin turned red with rage.

Lyndz, Rosie and I didn't do too badly either. Lyndz's effort was a bit feeble and only just made it over the net, but Rosie and I hit ours pretty hard, even though Rosie's was a bit high. We had another couple of goes, and then Mark came over to speak to us again.

The Sleepover Club

"Right, I want you to go back on to the courts and practise those forehands," he said. "Oh, and before you go, I want to tell you all about the tournament we'll be having at the end of the week."

Tournament? We looked at each other. That sounded interesting.

"We'll be finishing the summer school with a doubles tennis tournament," Mark went on. "So you'll need to get into pairs, and let me know who you'll be playing with. Now off you go."

The Queen and the Goblin were looking smugly at each other.

"I reckon we've got a great chance of winning that, Emily," the Queen said gleefully. "There's no one here who's as good as we are."

"We'll walk it!" the Goblin chortled. "Especially as we'll be able to practise at Green Lawns every afternoon."

Kenny turned to the rest of us, as the M&Ms went off, grinning from ear to ear. "Did you hear that?" she said urgently. "We can't let them win!"

"We'd better start practising then," Rosie said. "Because at the moment, Fliss is the only one of us who's any good."

Sleepover Girls on the Ball

"Hang on a minute," I cut in. "We've got another problem to sort out first."

"What's that?" Fliss asked.

"It's a *doubles* tournament, and we need to get into pairs," I pointed out. "Do the maths. There's *five* of us…"

CHAPTER FOUR

Everyone's faces dropped.

"Maybe one of us could play with someone else," Lyndz said hopefully.

I shook my head. "No, remember I said that there were seventeen of us? That means one person's always going to be left over."

"And it looks like that's going to be one of us," Kenny said gloomily, "because everyone else is already in twos."

"What are we going to do?" Fliss asked.

"I'll drop out," Lyndz offered bravely. "I'm rubbish anyway."

"You're no worse than me," Rosie argued.

"Or me," I said.

Sleepover Girls on the Ball

"We could spin for it," Fliss suggested, twirling her tennis racket on the ground to show us what she meant. "That's the fairest way to choose the lucky four."

We all nodded. So we gathered round in a circle, and Fliss spun her racket. It came to a stop, pointing at Lyndz.

"OK, Lyndz, you're in," said Kenny. "And now for your partner."

The next spin left the racket pointing at Rosie.

"You two are a team then," said Fliss. She looked really envious. I was pretty jealous too because I really wanted to play. Once we'd stopped messing about and started playing properly, I was surprised by how much I'd enjoyed myself.

"Lyndz, you spin it now," Kenny said. "And then it'll be fair."

Lyndz spun the racket, and it ended up pointing at Fliss. Fliss tried not to look too pleased.

"So it's between me and Frankie," Kenny said.

My heart was pounding as Lyndz spun the racket again. It stopped really slowly, and pointed straight at…

47

The Sleepover Club

Kenny.

"Sorry, Frankie," said Fliss and Rosie together.

"Poor old Frankie," said Lyndz sympathetically.

"Yeah, bad luck, Frankie." Kenny thumped me on the back.

"It's cool," I said, trying not to sound like I minded too much. "You're a better player than me, anyway."

"Come on, girls." Mark was calling and waving at us from another court. "You should be practising your forehands."

We spread out across our court, and began knocking the ball to each other. I didn't feel much like playing any more, but I didn't want to let the others down. After all, they had to practise if they were going to beat the M&Ms.

Fliss hit a forehand drive towards Kenny, who ran forward to return it. At just that moment, Emily Berryman came charging on to our court, chasing a stray ball. Kenny bashed straight into her, and knocked the Goblin flying.

"Help!" Emily shrieked, as she fell backwards on to her bottom. "You did that on purpose, Laura McKenzie!"

Sleepover Girls on the Ball

"No, I didn't," Kenny retorted. "*You* got in *my* way."

The Queen came stomping over to stick her nose in, as usual.

"You're just trying to make sure we don't win the tournament," she snapped, hauling the Goblin to her feet. "You tried to injure Emily by pushing her over!"

"Oh, go stuff a tennis ball in your mouth!" Kenny replied. "On second thoughts, try two tennis balls – your mouth's big enough."

"You won't be laughing when we win that tournament," the Queen said threateningly, and she stalked off, dragging the Goblin behind her.

"The trouble is, they *could* win it," Kenny muttered. "They're good."

"And did you hear Emily say that they were going to practise every afternoon at that posh tennis club?" Rosie said gloomily.

"Well, we can practise too," I pointed out. "We don't need a posh club. We've all got gardens. Or we could go to the park."

The others cheered up a bit. Although I wasn't going to be playing in the tournament, I reckoned it was going to be a full-time job keeping the others from getting too depressed!

49

The Sleepover Club

We went back to practising our forehands, and then Mark called us all together again. This time he showed us how to serve properly. And guess what? Surprise, surprise (and nobody was more surprised than ME), I turned out to be quite good at it. I banged down quite a few good serves, and everyone (except the M&Ms) looked pretty impressed.

"Frankie, maybe you *should* be playing in the tournament," Lyndz said, when we'd been sent off to practise on our own again. "I don't mind dropping out."

I shook my head. "Nope, you were all chosen fair and square."

"I don't think me and Lyndz have got much of a hope," Rosie said. "I'm rubbish."

"No, I'm worse than you," Lyndz argued.

"No, *I'm* the worst player."

"No, I am."

"Shut up, you two," Kenny said, giving them both a shove.

"Kenny and Fliss are in with a good chance," I said. "Fliss is brilliant."

Fliss turned pink with pleasure.

"What about me?" Kenny demanded.

Sleepover Girls on the Ball

"You'll be all right, as long as you don't fool around," Fliss said sternly.

"Me? Fool around?" Kenny snorted. "Do I ever?"

"Yes!" we all shouted, and pelted her with tennis balls.

About ten minutes later, Mark announced that it was the end of the coaching session for today. None of us wanted to go home though – we could have stayed there and played all day long!

"There's my mum and Auntie Jill," Fliss said, as we put the tennis balls in the boxes.

"Hurry up, Emily," called the Queen in a loud voice which just about everyone could hear. "My mum will be here soon to take us over to Green Lawns."

"They're really getting on my nerves, going on about that tennis club," Kenny muttered. She did a double-take in the direction of Mrs Proudlove. "Hey, what's the matter with your mum and Auntie Jill, Fliss? They look like they've won the lottery!"

Mrs Proudlove and Auntie Jill were hurrying towards the tennis courts, looking really excited. We went to meet them. So did Mark.

The Sleepover Club

"We're in!" Mrs Proudlove announced. She was waving a small piece of card in the air. "We just heard this morning."

"In what?" Kenny asked, looking puzzled.

"The Green Lawns Tennis Club," Auntie Jill said triumphantly, showing us her membership card. She flung her arms around Mark and gave him a hug. "Thanks for putting in a good word for us."

"That's great," Mark said.

"Excellent!" Fliss beamed. "I'll be able to practise there too, for the tournament."

"Are you ready, girls?" Mrs Proudlove called. "Jill and I want to go to the tennis club this afternoon, and I have to take you all home first."

Kenny nudged me. "What do you reckon?" she whispered in my ear.

I blinked at her. "What're you talking about?"

Kenny grinned at the rest of us. "How annoyed do you think the M&Ms would be if the whole of the Sleepover Club turned up at their posh tennis club this afternoon?"

"They'd go totally mad," I said. "But it's not very likely to happen, is it?"

"We're not members," Rosie pointed out, looking puzzled. "They only let members in."

Sleepover Girls on the Ball

"*We're* not members." Kenny winked at us. "But Fliss's mum and Auntie Jill are – and you heard what Fliss said before. They can take guests!"

Fliss turned a sickly shade of white, while Rosie, Lyndz and I burst out laughing.

"Do you really think my mum is going to let us all go to the club with her this afternoon?" Fliss spluttered. "Dream on, Kenny!"

Kenny grinned. "Why not? We can ask her, can't we?"

"You can ask her, but she won't say yes!" I replied. "Not in a million years."

The M&Ms were sitting on the bench near us, changing their shoes. Now they got up, and picked up their bags.

"Come on, Emily," said the Queen, shooting us a poisonous sideways glare. "Let's go. At least we'll be able to have a *proper* game at Green Lawns without stupid people mucking about."

Kenny gave them a cheery wave. "We'll see you there!" she called.

The Queen's mouth fell open as she goggled at us.

"*What* did you say?" she roared.

"We're coming to the tennis club this afternoon," Kenny retorted coolly. "We're going to be there regularly from now on."

Emma Hughes couldn't think of a single thing to say. She turned bright red with rage and stomped off, with Emily scurrying along behind her.

"Oh, Kenny, what've you done?" Fliss moaned, looking terrified. "I am *not* asking my mum if she'll take us to the tennis club!"

"Calm down, Flissy," Kenny said breezily. "I'll ask her myself."

CHAPTER FIVE

"Oh, no," said Fliss's mum, folding her arms. "I don't think that's a good idea at all."

"Why not?" Kenny said, trying to look all innocent. "We wouldn't be any trouble."

Mrs Proudlove looked even more doubtful. "Yes, well..." she said. "I've heard *that* before."

"Oh, go on," Kenny nagged her. "We'd only sit and watch. We wouldn't *do* anything."

"And maybe we could learn something by watching you and Auntie Jill," I added. "Then we could get better at tennis ourselves." OK, so I was doing some serious sucking-up here. But if we didn't turn up at the club now, after everything Kenny had said to the M&Ms, we'd look like prize prats.

"Oh, that would be great," Rosie said, joining in to help me out. "I'm so rubbish at tennis. I bet I'd be loads better if I could watch someone *really* good."

"Me too," Lyndz added.

"And you and Auntie Jill are brilliant at tennis," Fliss finished up.

"Well, I don't know about that." But Fliss's mum looked pleased. She turned to Auntie Jill. "What do you think?"

"Oh, let them come," said Auntie Jill with a smile. "There's two of us to keep an eye on them, after all. And they can't get up to much, if they're just sitting watching us play."

"Well, all right then," Mrs Proudlove said, and we all cheered. "But I'm warning you," she went on sternly, "I don't want *any* messing around." She stared hard at us. "We've waited a long time to get into this club, and we don't want anything going wrong. Is that clear?"

We all nodded.

"I'll see you there later," Mark said, kissing Auntie Jill on the cheek. "'Bye, girls."

"Yes!" Kenny said triumphantly, as we hurried over to the Proudloves' people carrier. "I knew we could swing it!"

"You heard what Mum said, Kenny," Fliss reminded her. "If we get into any trouble, I'm dead – and so are the rest of you."

"We'll all be really good," I said. "Won't we, Kenny?"

"Yep, cross my heart and hope to die," Kenny said loudly. "Unless the M&Ms annoy me, of course," she added under her breath.

Mrs Proudlove drove us all home, and dropped us off one by one, after she'd arranged to pick us up in an hour or two.

"Mum!" I dashed into the house, yelling my head off. "Mum, is lunch ready? And is it OK if I go out this afternoon? Fliss's mum is taking us to her tennis club."

My mum was working in the study, with Izzy in the playpen next to her. She looked up from the computer and stared at me.

"A tennis club? I thought you hated tennis, and you were only going to the coaching sessions because Fliss forced you into it?"

"Oh, Mum, you're *so* out of date!" I groaned. "Tennis is *cool*."

The Sleepover Club

Fliss's mum turned up again bang on two o'clock to pick me up. She'd already collected the others, so I dived into the back of the people carrier to join them.

"I was just saying," Mrs Proudlove remarked, as she pulled away from the kerb, "that I expect you all to be on your best behaviour, and not to show me up."

"This is worse than going on a school trip!" Kenny whispered in my ear. "We've been getting the big lecture for the last five minutes."

Auntie Jill, who was in the front seat, turned round and winked at us. "I'm sure they'll be fine," she said.

The Green Lawns Tennis Club was just outside Cuddington, in the countryside. I'd been past it and seen the big iron gates loads of times, but I'd never been in before. There was a large car park at the front, and large, brightly-coloured flowerbeds.

"Right, you can get out," said Mrs Proudlove, switching off the engine. "But stay together where I can keep an eye on you."

"Does she want us to hold hands like five-year-olds?" Kenny grumbled.

Sleepover Girls on the Ball

We went over to the entrance. Fliss's mum insisted on walking in front, and she kept looking round at us nervously, as if she thought we were already up to something. There was a turnstile next to a little green-roofed hut, and a man with a big moustache and grey hair was sitting inside the hut, reading a newspaper. He glared suspiciously at us.

"Members only," he snapped. "Membership cards?"

"Oh, yes, of course," said Mrs Proudlove. She and Auntie Jill held theirs out, and the man took them. "And these girls are our guests," she added.

The man looked down his nose at us as if we were a bad smell.

"Nobody's allowed to play on our courts unless they're wearing white," he said, giving Kenny's football strip a disgusted glance.

"They're not playing," Fliss's mum said quickly. "Just watching."

The man didn't want to let us into the club at all. He handed the membership cards back really slowly, after he'd spent ages looking at them, and then he operated the turnstile, grumbling all the time to himself.

The Sleepover Club

"He's a real misery-guts, isn't he?" Kenny said, as we went through. "I've seen more cheerful people at funerals!"

"Hey, this is pretty cool," I said, looking around.

The tennis club was really big. There were lots of courts, and quite a few people were playing on them. There were landscaped gardens around the courts, filled with flowers, and there was a fountain too, of a boy riding on a dolphin. In the middle of it all was a big clubhouse, next to a posh-looking restaurant with tables set outside on a patio. We were all pretty impressed.

Rosie pointed at a poster pinned to the clubhouse door. "Look at that. That's what the M&Ms were going on about last week."

**COME AND CELEBRATE 50 YEARS OF
THE GREEN LAWNS TENNIS CLUB!**

A SPECIAL GALA AFTERNOON ON JULY 29th

**EXHIBITION MATCHES
REFRESHMENTS PROVIDED
ALL MEMBERS WELCOME!**

Sleepover Girls on the Ball

"That's in two days' time," Fliss said eagerly. "Maybe Mum will bring us to that."

"That would really get up the M&Ms' noses!" Kenny grinned.

"I have to pop into the clubhouse, and find out which court we're playing on," Fliss's mum said. She fixed us all with a laser-beam stare. "Don't move, or touch anything while I'm gone."

We stood outside the clubhouse with Auntie Jill, staring at everything going on around us.

"I wonder if the M&Ms are here yet," Rosie said.

"Maybe we can have a wander round the courts, and find out," Kenny began, but she shut up when Auntie Jill gave her a look. "Oh, I forgot. We're not allowed to move!"

Fliss's mum came back. "Court Seven," she said to Auntie Jill. "Let's go and get changed."

We went over to Court 7. We looked at all the other courts we passed on the way, but there was no sign of the M&Ms.

"Maybe they haven't arrived yet," Lyndz suggested, as we reached the changing-rooms.

"You girls had better come with us while we get changed, so that we can keep an eye on you," Mrs Proudlove began, but then she stopped as Auntie Jill pointed at a sign on the door.

ONLY PLAYERS ARE ALLOWED IN THE CHANGING-ROOMS

"Oh." Fliss's mum looked worried. "You'll have to stay outside then. But—"

"We know," said Kenny. "Don't move!"

"Can't we go on to Court Seven, and wait for you there, Mum?" Fliss asked.

Mrs Proudlove glared at her. "No, Felicity, you stay right here," she snapped, and she and Auntie Jill went into the changing-rooms.

We all stood there, shuffling our feet for a few moments and getting really bored. Then Kenny started walking towards the tennis courts, which were right ahead of us.

"Kenny!" Fliss began to panic. "Come back!"

"Don't get your knickers in a twist, Fliss," Kenny said impatiently. She leaned against the fence and peered into the nearest court. "Is this ours? Because it looks like someone's playing

Sleepover Girls on the Ball

on here already. There's some rackets and tennis balls lying on the ground."

I went over to her. "No, that's Court Eight," I said, squinting at the number on the fence. "Ours must be the next one."

"Frankie, come back," Fliss wailed, but I didn't take any notice. After all, we were only about two metres away from her!

"Hey, what about a knock-up?" Kenny nudged me, and nodded at Court 8.

"Not a good idea, Kenny." I shook my head. "Fliss's mum would go mad."

Kenny shrugged. "Oh, she'll be ages yet. And anyway, why would someone leave tennis rackets and balls lying around, if they didn't want people to use them?"

"Kenny," I said warningly as she pushed open the door of the court, but that didn't stop her. She walked in, and picked up one of the rackets.

"Kenny, what're you doing?" Lyndz said. She and Rosie hurried over to join us, with Fliss trailing after them looking terrified. "Put that down!"

"It's OK," Kenny grinned. She brought the racket over to the fence and showed it to us.

"This racket is *really* gross. I'm sure no one would mind if we had a game with it."

Kenny was right, the racket was really awful. The strings weren't broken, but it was made of wood, not like Mrs Proudlove's posh metal one, and nearly all the paint had flaked off.

"Come on, who's going to play against me?" Kenny asked, waving the racket around as she tried out her shots.

The rest of us looked at each other. We weren't quite as brave as Kenny. None of us wanted to annoy Fliss's mum.

"You lot are so boring!" Kenny announced. "Hey, have you seen what some of the players do when they win a match at Wimbledon? They throw their rackets right up into the air."

"How do you know?" I asked. "I thought you hated tennis until this morning!"

"Well, I've seen the *end* of some of the matches, haven't I?" Kenny retorted. "You know, while I was waiting for *EastEnders* to come on."

"What happens when the rackets fall down again?" Rosie asked. "Do they catch them or what?"

Sleepover Girls on the Ball

"What if they don't get out of the way in time, and it hits them on the head?" Lyndz wanted to know.

Kenny considered that. "I dunno," she said. "Let's give it a go!"

"Kenny, no!" Fliss yelled, but it was too late. Kenny had flung the racket into the air as hard as she could.

"Don't worry, Fliss," Kenny called, "I'll catch it on the way down."

The racket started hurtling downwards.

"Kenny, you're not going to catch it!" I shouted. "Get out of the way!"

Kenny looked alarmed at the speed with which the racket was falling. She leapt out of the way, and the racket hit the hard surface of the court.

CR-R-R-ACK!

We all stared in horror. The wooden frame of the racket had split.

"What's going on here?" said a loud voice behind us.

Luckily, it wasn't Mrs Proudlove. Instead, a tall, plump woman with grey hair, wearing tennis whites, was marching towards us, followed by a much weedier woman of about the same age, who looked really scared. Not as scared as we were, though!

Before any of us had a chance to say anything, the tall woman spotted her broken racket lying on the ground.

"My racket!" she roared furiously, hurrying on to the tennis court. She snatched it up, inspected the damage and glared at Kenny, red-faced. "My lucky racket, the one my Aunt Fiona played with at Wimbledon in 1951!"

"Oh," Kenny said politely. "I'm really sorry, but maybe it was time you got a new one anyway, then."

She was trying to be helpful, but the woman almost had a fit.

"How dare you!" she shouted, waving the racket at Kenny. "This is part of my family's history!"

"Steady on, Dorothy," said the other woman in a wobbly voice. I think she was as frightened of her friend as we were!

"We're really, really sorry," Fliss stammered, looking as if she was about to faint with fright.

"Do you know who I am?" The woman glared round at us. "I'm Mrs Morgan, the club

Sleepover Girls on the Ball

secretary. And I'm going to make sure you never set foot in Green Lawns again!"

CHAPTER SIX

"Well, how was I supposed to know that the racket belonged to the club secretary?" Kenny moaned in a low voice. "I mean, it was really tatty. I didn't think anyone would mind if I played with it."

"Ssh, Fliss's mum is looking at us," Rosie hissed.

Mrs Proudlove was glaring at us in the driver's mirror, so we all shut up. The atmosphere in the car was colder and frostier than the North Pole. While Mrs Morgan had been telling us off, Fliss's mum and Auntie Jill had come out of the changing-rooms just in time to find out what had happened. Mrs

Sleepover Girls on the Ball

Morgan gave *them* an earful too. Fliss's mum had been so furious and embarrassed, she'd hauled us off home straight away without even bothering to change. Now we were pretty much in doom forever.

"It's a wonder Mrs Morgan didn't throw us out of the club there and then," Fliss's mum said through her teeth.

"I think she only let us off because she knows I'm Mark's girlfriend," Auntie Jill muttered.

"I don't know if I'll ever be able to show my face there again," Mrs Proudlove groaned, changing gear with a lot of crunching and banging. "I certainly won't be going there for the next few days."

"Me neither," said Auntie Jill.

"Sorry," Kenny said again, for about the millionth time. "But that racket was just *lying* there. She shouldn't have left it lying around if it was that important."

Auntie Jill turned round, and directed an icy stare at Kenny. "Everyone at Green Lawns knows about Mrs Morgan's special racket," she said. "And nobody would *dare* to touch it. The reason why it was lying on the court was that

Mrs Morgan and her friend were about to have a game."

"Sorry," Kenny muttered again.

"I knew this would happen," Fliss's mum grumbled. "Well, that's it." She shot us another glare in the mirror. "None of you will be coming to Green Lawns with me ever again. Is that clear?"

"But, Mum—" Fliss began.

"Is that *clear*?" Mrs Proudlove said again in a louder voice.

We nodded. We didn't dare to speak, not even to each other, but I knew what everyone else was thinking. We'd been boasting to the M&Ms about how we were going to be practising at the tennis club from now on. If they didn't see us there, we'd never hear the end of it…

"Look, there are the M&Ms waiting for us," Fliss said gloomily, as we drove through the college grounds.

"Are those girls friends of yours?" asked my dad, who was dropping us off. Mrs Proudlove had refused to give us a lift after what had happened the day before.

Sleepover Girls on the Ball

We all made being-sick noises.

"Dad, we ARE not friends with those two losers," I told him.

"So why are they waiting for you then?" Dad said.

I rolled my eyes. "Don't ask."

"I don't think I want to know," my dad said with a grin. "See you at lunchtime."

We all climbed slowly out of the car. The M&Ms were watching us gleefully, just waiting to find out why we hadn't been playing at the club yesterday after all Kenny's boasting.

"Look, we'll just say we were there, and they didn't see us," Kenny hissed.

"Well, we *were* there – for about ten minutes!" Lyndz pointed out. "So it's not really a fib."

"You don't think the Queen and the Goblin heard about what happened to Mrs Morgan's racket, do you?" Fliss squeaked, looking really worried.

Kenny groaned. "I hope not – they'll laugh their heads off if they know it was us."

"If they know it was *you*, you mean," Fliss said grumpily. She was in a bit of a bad mood this morning. Her mum must have had a right go at her.

"Not wearing your magic cloaks today, then," the Queen called as we walked on to the court.

We all stared at her. None of us had a clue what she was going on about.

"Your magic cloaks," the Queen repeated. The Goblin was sniggering away beside her. "You know, the ones that make you *invisible*."

"Yeah, because if you were at the club yesterday afternoon, you *must* have been invisible," Emily Berryman explained sarcastically. "Because *we* didn't see you!"

"We were there," Kenny said shortly. "We had a quick game, and then we left."

"Oh, yeah, right," the Goblin chortled. "You must think we're stupid!"

"We do, actually," I chimed in.

"You didn't go to the club!" Emma Hughes said. "I knew you were making it all up."

"We're not," Kenny snapped. "Actually we're going to be there this afternoon as well!"

"What?" I muttered. "Kenny, what're you talking about?"

"We're going to the club this afternoon, right?" Kenny turned round and eyeballed the rest of us really hard.

Sleepover Girls on the Ball

"Er – yeah..." we all muttered. Fliss was looking nervous, and I didn't blame her. Kenny and her big mouth had gone and dropped us right in it *again*!

"Are you totally and completely bonkers, Kenny?" I demanded, when the M&Ms had stomped off, looking a bit less smug. "There's no way we can get into that club again!"

"My mum won't take us," Fliss said anxiously. "She'll kill me if I ask her."

"And we're not members, so how can we get in?" Rosie added.

"Kenny, what have you done!" Lyndz groaned.

"Leave it with me." Kenny grabbed a racket, as Mark came over to join us. "I'll have a think about it, and I'll come up with one of my super-duper, fantastically cool ideas."

"You mean, you'll think of a way to get us into even more trouble," Fliss said gloomily.

Mark gave us all a talk to start with, reminding us of what we'd learned yesterday. We lined up and did some more forehand practice shots, then he sent us off to practise against each other.

The Sleepover Club

Things went a bit better than yesterday. Even Rosie managed not to hit the ball right over the fence this time. The most difficult thing was trying to hit the ball hard and still keep it within the white lines. Kenny could whack the ball really hard, but she kept knocking it out of the court.

Mark came over to give us some advice.

"Remember what I said yesterday," he told us. "The forehand can be a really easy shot, but if you want to be a good player, there are some things you need to remember. You have to think about your grip, and the position of your racket when you hit the ball." He took Rosie's racket from her to show us what he meant. "Move the racket back as fast as you can, to get ready for the shot, and keep it vertical. And try to finish up with your racket pointing towards the place you want the ball to go."

"There's so much to remember," Kenny groaned, as Mark went off again.

"And you thought tennis was just about hitting a ball over a net!" I reminded her.

The morning went by really quickly. We were getting so into the game that we didn't take any notice of the M&Ms, who were playing on the same court as Ryan and Danny again. But when the session was over, they started hanging around as we packed up the rackets and balls, smirking all over their faces.

"So we'll see you this afternoon," the Queen said loudly. "At the club."

Kenny glared at her. "That's right."

"Don't bring your magic cloaks this time then," the Goblin chortled, "or we won't be able to see you!"

And off they went, laughing like drains.

I looked at Kenny. "So what's your big idea then?" I asked. "If you've got one at all!"

"'Course I've got an idea." Kenny was looking well pleased with herself, which usually means trouble. "We're going to get into that club, no problem."

"How?" Lyndz asked, looking puzzled.

"I'm not climbing over the fence!" Fliss said firmly.

"Don't be daft, Fliss," Kenny said. "We're not going to do *that*."

"So what *are* we going to do?" Rosie asked.

Kenny grinned. "Fliss is going to borrow her mum's membership card, pretend to be her mum and sign us all in as guests!"

CHAPTER SEVEN

"Kenny!" Fliss howled. "That's the most stupid idea I've ever heard!"

"Why?" Kenny asked crossly. "I thought it was brilliant, even though I say so myself."

"You've really gone bananas this time, Kenny," I told her. "It'll never work."

"How can I pretend to be my mum?" Fliss demanded. "She's twenty-eight!"

"So?" Kenny shrugged her shoulders. "Her age isn't on the membership card, is it? Just her name. You can easily call yourself Nicola Proudlove."

"Hang on," Rosie said. "I got a quick look at the card when we went to the club yesterday, and there's a photo of Fliss's mum on it."

"Oh, rats!" said Kenny. She thought for a minute, and then beamed at us. "OK, no problem. Fliss and her mum look like each other, and they've both got long blonde hair. Fliss can wear shades, and we'll put loads of make-up on her to make her look a bit older, and more like the photo."

"Yeah?" Fliss brightened up a bit, and stopped looking so nervous. She loves doing girly stuff with make-up. "Do you really think it'll work?"

"Of course it won't work!" I said, and Rosie and Lyndz nodded in agreement.

"Have you got a better idea, Francesca?" Kenny asked me.

I shook my head. "Nope."

"OK, then, so this is what we'll do," Kenny went on. "After lunch, we'll meet at Fliss's house, and get her all made up. Then we'll cycle to the club, so bring your bikes."

Fliss was looking nervous again. "I don't think my mum will be very pleased if you all come round to my place. She's still really annoyed about yesterday."

"Just tell her we're doing homework

together," Kenny said. "The oldies always like that."

"All right," Fliss agreed.

"See you all there then," Kenny grinned, as my dad drew up outside the tennis courts.

"Quick, get inside before my mum comes down to see who it is," Fliss whispered, hustling me through the door of the Proudloves' house. I'd left my bike outside in the front garden, along with the others which were already parked there. "She keeps checking up on us, so we have to pretend to be doing homework."

"Where *is* your mum?" I asked, stepping into the hall.

"She's with a client," Fliss replied, pushing me towards the stairs. Her mum is a beautician, and she has a sort of beauty salon in one of the spare bedrooms where she does all sorts of treatments. "Come on, we're in my room."

We tiptoed up the stairs, and Fliss opened her bedroom door.

"Yikes!" Kenny gasped, jumping a mile into the air. She was in the middle of tipping a make-

Sleepover Girls on the Ball

up bag full of lipsticks and nail varnishes on to the floor. "I thought you were Fliss's mum."

"Come on, let's get on with it," Fliss said, looking nervous.

"One of us had better be on guard," Rosie suggested.

"Good idea," I said. "I'll do it."

I went over to the door and opened it, so that I could see right down the landing.

"Now, which one do you think I should wear?" Fliss held up two lipsticks. She's got loads of make-up that her mum lets her wear when we're playing dressing-up or having fashion shows. "Peachy Kiss or Purple Pout?"

"Oh, Fliss!" Kenny groaned. "It doesn't matter. Just slap some lipstick on, and then we can go."

"Don't be silly, Kenny," Fliss retorted. "I've got to do it properly. My mum's taught me all about make-up."

"Peachy Kiss is nice," Lyndz said, twisting the lipstick up out of its tube.

"OK," Fliss agreed. "But I've got to do my blusher and mascara first."

We all sat around waiting as Fliss did her face. Kenny was so impatient, she couldn't sit

The Sleepover Club

still. She kept hopping around from foot to foot, like she wanted to go to the loo or something.

"OK, I'm all done." Fliss fluttered her eyelashes at us. "What do you think?"

"You *do* look a few years older," Rosie said.

"Fourteen, maybe." I added, "But not twenty-eight!"

"Yes, but Fliss's mum looks really young for her age, anyway," Kenny pointed out. "We'll get away with it."

"What if the man on the gate asks me how old I am?" Fliss said, looking panicky.

"Say you're fourteen," Kenny instructed her. "And if he says you look older in the photo, just tell him you were having a bad hair day when it was taken."

"I hope it's not the same man who was on the gate yesterday," Lyndz said suddenly. "He might remember us."

"We'll just have to risk it," Kenny said in a determined voice.

A door opened further down the landing. And I nearly died when I saw Fliss's mum come out and head in our direction.

"Mrs Proudlove's coming!" I hissed.

Sleepover Girls on the Ball

"Help!" Fliss gasped. "What about my make-up?"

"Lie down on the bed with your back to the door, and stick your head in a book," Kenny told her. Between the four of us, we bundled her on to the bed, and thrust a book into her hand. "And whatever you do, don't look up!"

By the time Fliss's mum opened the door, we were all sitting quietly and reading.

"Everything all right in here?" Mrs Proudlove asked suspiciously.

"Fine, thank you," we replied politely.

"Mum, we've finished our homework," Fliss mumbled without looking up. "Is it OK if we go out on our bikes now?"

Mrs Proudlove frowned. "I suppose so," she sighed. "But just *try* to stay out of trouble, please."

She went out again. We all heaved a sigh of relief.

"Come on, let's get going," Kenny said. "Fliss, have you got some sunglasses?"

Fliss nodded, and picked up a really funky pink, heart-shaped pair of shades. Then she grabbed her sports bag.

"How're we going to have a game, if we do get in?" I asked. "Fliss is the only one of us who's got a racket."

"Oh, we can always borrow one from somebody," Kenny replied.

"As long as it's not Mrs Morgan!" Rosie giggled nervously.

"We'd better make sure we stay out of her way," I said. "And Mark's too, just in case he tells Auntie Jill that he saw us there."

We went out of the bedroom.

"Don't forget the membership card," Kenny reminded Fliss.

"That'll be downstairs by the phone," Fliss said confidently. "My mum always keeps stuff like that there."

We all went down the stairs really quietly, just in case Mrs Proudlove came out to check on us again. Luckily, she didn't. Fliss stopped by the phone table in the hall, and quickly went through the letters and bits of paper which were lying there.

"It's not here!" she gasped.

"Oh no!" Kenny groaned. "Well, where else would it be?"

"It might be in my mum's sports bag," Fliss

Sleepover Girls on the Ball

said doubtfully. "Hang on, no, it isn't. I remember her saying that she'd emptied everything out."

"It could be *anywhere!*" Rosie said, looking around.

"I've seen it this morning." Fliss frowned, trying to remember. "I *know* I've seen it."

"Think, Fliss, think!" Kenny urged her.

We all stood around, while Fliss racked her brains.

"The kitchen!" Fliss said triumphantly, at last. "I saw it lying on the worktop."

We were just about to dash into the kitchen, when we all froze. A door had opened overhead, and there was the sound of footsteps.

"My mum must have finished with her client!" Fliss wailed. "If she sees me with all this make-up on, she'll guess we're up to something."

"Quick, we've got to get that card!" Kenny hissed.

Fliss ran into the kitchen. As we heard Mrs Proudlove and her client at the top of the stairs, Fliss dashed out again, waving the card in the air.

The Sleepover Club

"I've got it!"

"Let's get out of here," I said, and we all raced out of the front door.

We collected our bikes from the Proudloves' front garden, and cycled off to the tennis club. It was a really warm and sunny day, and we were all sweating a bit by the time we got there. Or maybe it was just nerves!

"I'm scared," Fliss moaned, as we locked our bikes up in the club car park.

"You'll be fine," Kenny said. "Just think about the M&Ms' faces when they see us inside the club."

"I hope they're there," I said. "Or this will all be a big waste of time."

"They'll be there," Kenny said.

We didn't go straight up to the entrance. Instead, we hung around on the edge of the car park, trying to see if the same man from yesterday was on duty.

"It's OK," Kenny said in a low voice. "It's a different guy."

We all marched up to the entrance. Fliss's knees were knocking together so much, though, we practically had to carry her.

"Membership cards, please." The man at the turnstile was a bit younger than the one from yesterday, and not quite so snooty.

"Er – yes." Fliss fumbled in her pocket. Her voice was a bit high and squeaky because she was nervous. "I'm a member, and these are my guests."

The man took the card and looked at it for what seemed like ages.

"You're Nicola Proudlove?" he said at last.

"Um – yes," Fliss muttered.

The man eyeballed Fliss sternly. "How old are you?" he asked.

"I'm fourteen," Fliss said in a wobbly voice.

"Oh, really." The man turned the membership card round, and held it out so that we could see it. "And how long have you been married, *Mrs* Proudlove?"

We all squinted at the card. There, next to the photo, it said *Mrs Nicola Proudlove*.

"Goodbye, Mrs Proudlove," said the man sarcastically. "And just make sure you give that card back to its rightful owner."

We all trailed gloomily back to the car park.

"Why didn't anyone notice the card said *Mrs* Proudlove?" I asked, glaring at Fliss.

"I didn't have time to look at it properly," Fliss snapped. "I was in too much of a rush."

"So the M&Ms win again," Rosie said.

"Maybe we should just give up," Lyndz suggested.

"Give up!" Kenny spluttered. "What do you mean, give up? I've just thought of another *brilliant* idea!"

CHAPTER EIGHT

We all groaned.

"Kenny, you're not serious!" I said.

"You haven't heard my idea yet," Kenny said indignantly. She took the membership card from Fliss, and waved it at us. "See this? How about if we make our *own* membership cards?"

"What, fake them, you mean?" Lyndz gasped.

Kenny nodded. "Look at this card," she said. "For a posh club, it's pretty ropey. I reckon we could copy it, no problem."

"That sounds a bit dodgy," I remarked.

"It's got to be against the law!" Fliss wailed.

The Sleepover Club

"Don't be a bunch of wimps," Kenny retorted. "We're not doing anything wrong. Not really."

"How do you work that one out?" I asked.

"Because all we're going to do is hang around inside the club until the M&Ms have seen us," Kenny replied. "It's not like we're going to nick anything or cause trouble."

"How about if someone spots us and realises we're not members?" Rosie asked. "Like that Mrs Morgan, for instance."

"Or Mark," I added.

Kenny grinned. "That's why my plan's so cool." She pointed at a poster for the gala afternoon, which was stuck on the fence. "Look, this is on tomorrow. There's going to be loads of members there, and I bet there'll be a lot of people who've come as guests too. So we aren't going to stand out in such a big crowd."

"I suppose not," Fliss said doubtfully.

"We won't be able to bag a court to have a game, though," I said. "No way. If there's going to be loads of people there, I bet all the courts will be booked, anyway."

"Yeah, we'd better not draw any attention to ourselves," Lyndz said, and the others nodded.

Sleepover Girls on the Ball

"OK, we'll just hang around until the M&Ms have seen us, and then we'll leg it," Kenny said.

"We'll need some photos if we're going to copy those membership cards," Rosie pointed out.

"There's a photo booth in the Post Office in the High Street," Kenny replied, jumping on her bike. "Come on!"

We all pedalled after her. We cycled back into Cuddington, and left our bikes in the car park behind the supermarket. The Post Office was right next door.

"Look, it's £3.50 for five photos," Kenny said, nodding at the photo booth. "How much money have we got?"

We all turned out our pockets. We had exactly £3.50 between us.

"See? This is our lucky day!" Kenny grinned. "Who's going first?"

"Wait a minute," I said. "How are we going to get in and out of the booth quick enough?"

"Just don't hang about," Kenny ordered us. "As soon as the flash goes off, get out of there as fast as you can. Frankie, you go first."

I went in and pulled the curtain. Then I sat down and adjusted the stool so that my face was in the middle of the little square in front of me.

"Don't have the stool too low." Kenny stuck her face round the curtain all of a sudden, nearly giving me a heart attack. "We won't have time to adjust it, and we're not all beanpoles like you!"

I put the stool up a bit higher, and started to put the money into the slot.

"Ready?" I called.

"Ready!" the others called back.

I dropped the last coin into the slot, and put on this really cheesy grin. I thought the flash was never going to come, but when it did, I jumped straight up. At the same moment, Kenny came hurtling through the curtain like Superman, and we banged heads.

"Aaargh!" Kenny groaned. "Get out of my way, you idiot!"

I fought my way past the curtain, and got out just in time before the second flash went off.

"You're next, Fliss," Rosie said, giving her a shove.

Looking flustered, Fliss hurried into the booth. We heard Kenny shout "*OW!*", and then

Sleepover Girls on the Ball

she hopped out of the booth, clutching her foot. "Fliss trod on my toe," she moaned.

"Go on, Rosie," Lyndz said, as the flash went off again.

Rosie pulled the curtain aside. Fliss was down on her knees, hunting around on the floor.

"I dropped my sunglasses," she gasped.

"Stay down, Fliss!" I told her. Rosie crammed on to the stool, trying not to tread on Fliss, who was crouched in a ball. The flash went off, and both of them hurried out. Lyndz dashed in, and just about got there in time to have her picture taken.

"What did you say about this being our lucky day?" I remarked to Kenny, who was clutching her head and rubbing her foot.

"Here are the photos," Fliss announced.

We all crowded round to take a look as the photos popped out of the machine. They were really and truly gruesome. I'd put the stool a bit too high, and the top of my head had been cut off. Kenny was pulling a face like she was in agony, which she probably was after we'd banged into each other. Fliss looked totally panicked, and Rosie was all

The Sleepover Club

hunched up because she was trying not to step on Fliss. Only Lyndz looked in any way normal.

"If they let us in with these, they must be mad," Rosie said. "We look awful!"

"We've got to make the cards now," Kenny said. "Whose place shall we go to?"

"Somewhere the oldies won't interfere and want to know what we're up to," I suggested. "So my place is out. My mum's got eyes in the back of her head."

"Not mine either," Fliss said quickly. "My mum keeps checking up on us."

"We could go to my house," Rosie said. "Tiff's got a holiday job, so she won't be there, and Adam's gone to summer camp." Adam and Tiffany are Rosie's brother and sister. "My mum'll be there, but she'll be studying."

"OK, let's go then." Kenny glanced at her watch. "We'll have to get a move on. Mum told me I had to be home by four."

We grabbed our bikes and pedalled like the wind to Rosie's house, which luckily was quite close by. Mrs Cartwright was working on the computer, and she just popped out to say hello, then left us to it. We scooted out into the

Sleepover Girls on the Ball

garden, while Rosie went to get us some drinks and something to eat. We really needed it, after the afternoon we'd had!

"Right, we need card, black felt pens, scissors and glue," Kenny said, ticking the items off on her fingers.

"Look, Fliss's mum's card is covered in this kind of clear plastic to protect it," I said. "How are we going to do that?"

"We've got some clear sticky-back plastic," Rosie said, coming out with a tray of orange squash and a family-sized bag of cheese and onion crisps. "My mum uses it to cover her college books."

"Excellent," Kenny said. We were sitting round the garden table, and she put Mrs Proudlove's card in the centre, so that we could all see it. "Now remember, it has to be exactly the same size and everything."

Rosie fetched the stuff we needed, and we got to work. Like Kenny had said, the cards weren't that posh-looking. They were just plain white with Green Lawns Tennis Club in black letters at the top, and they had the member's photo, name and signature on the front. I'd thought that Kenny's idea was really daft, but I was surprised by how good the cards looked as we worked on them.

"Rats," Kenny said, looking at her watch. "I've got to go. I'll have to finish mine at home."

"Me too," I said, slipping the card into my pocket.

Fliss and Lyndz decided it was about time they went home as well. Rosie cut us some squares of sticky-back plastic so that we could finish the cards off that evening, and then we went to get our bikes.

"What happens if we don't get into the club tomorrow?" Lyndz asked.

"I'll think of another plan!" Kenny said firmly. "I'm not letting the M&Ms think they've got one over on us..."

"You can play a backhand with one or two hands," Mark said, and held up his tennis racket, showing us the different ways to hold it. It was the following morning, and we were at our coaching session. Lyndz's mum had taken us, and she was a bit late picking us up, so we'd got there just as Mark had started the session off. At least that meant that we didn't have to

Sleepover Girls on the Ball

put up with the M&Ms going on at us. They'd just sniggered and nudged each other when we'd arrived.

"There are a few important things to try and remember, whether you play a one-handed or two-handed shot," Mark went on. "Hold the racket head straight. If you tilt it slightly, you can get backspin on the ball, but for the moment just practise keeping it straight."

Someone poked me in the back. I glanced round, and Emma Hughes and Emily Berryman grinned unpleasantly at me.

"I thought you were going to the club yesterday afternoon," the Queen said.

"We did," I replied. No need to say we hadn't actually gone in!

"You didn't," Emily said accusingly. "We were there for most of the afternoon, and we didn't see you."

"Well, you must need glasses then," I retorted, and turned away.

"You lot are big fat liars!" the Queen said. "You're not members, and you've never been there at all!"

"Yes, we have." Kenny joined in. "And we're going to be at the gala afternoon today, too."

The Sleepover Club

"Huh! I'll believe that when I see it," Emma Hughes snorted.

"Emma, could you be quiet please?" Mark said sharply, and the Queen turned bright red.

We spent the session practising our backhands, and then Mark let us actually have a proper game for the last hour, with scoring and everything. He gave us each a sheet of paper, which explained exactly how to do it. Some of the others played doubles, but we decided to play singles and take it in turns to play each other, although we had to limit each match to just three games.

Of course, Fliss was easily the best, and she beat the pants off all of us, but Kenny was good too (when she wasn't belting the ball right out of the court and giving points away), and I wasn't too bad either. My serve was quite good, but I couldn't hit the ball as hard as Kenny. Rosie and Lyndz were OK too, although they weren't as good as Fliss and Kenny.

"I think you and Kenny might have a chance of winning the tournament on Friday," I said, as we packed away when the coaching session was over.

Sleepover Girls on the Ball

"Yeah, if I can stop losing points by whacking the ball out of play," Kenny grumbled.

"You just need a bit more practice," Fliss said.

"Well, we've only got today and tomorrow, and then the tournament's on Friday," Kenny pointed out.

"The M&Ms aren't as good as they think they are, though," Rosie chimed in. "I was watching them today, and Emily's really weedy."

"Yeah, she didn't return half the shots, and Emma was telling her off," Lyndz added.

Kenny waved at the M&Ms as they went past. "See you at the gala afternoon," she called.

"Oh, shut up," the Queen snapped. "If you think you can wind us up by always pretending you're there when you're not, it won't work!"

"Yeah, we *know* you're making it up," the Goblin added.

The Queen turned to her. "Tell you what, Em," she said. "If we don't see them there this afternoon, we'll ask Mrs Morgan, the club secretary, if she knows them."

"Ooh, that's a good idea," the Goblin said, and they walked off.

The Sleepover Club

"Did you hear that?" I hissed. "If the M&Ms speak to Mrs Morgan, she might tell them that we're the ones who broke her racket."

"The M&Ms would love that," Kenny groaned. "So we've got to make sure we get into that club this afternoon!"

We arranged to meet up at my place, ready to cycle to the tennis club later. Then we hung around, waiting for Lyndz's mum. Mrs Cartwright was late again picking us up, so when I got home, lunch was ready. I quickly got changed, and I'd just sat down and picked up my cheese and pickle sandwich when the phone rang. My mum went to answer it, and came back, looking suspicious.

"It's Fliss for you," she said, "and she sounds in a right old flap. Are you girls up to something?"

"'Course not, Mum," I said airily. "You know what Fliss is like. She panics about *everything*."

I waited till my mum had gone back into the kitchen, and then I dashed into the hall.

"Frankie?" Fliss squealed, nearly deafening me. "You'll never guess what's happened!"

Sleepover Girls on the Ball

"What?" I asked.

"My mum and Auntie Jill have decided to go to the tennis club this afternoon!" Fliss wailed.

CHAPTER NINE

"Oh, you're joking!" I groaned. "I thought they were too embarrassed to go after what happened?"

"Yeah, that's what they *said*," Fliss replied. "But then Mum said there'd be loads of people there for the gala thing, so maybe it wouldn't be so embarrassing. And Mark's talked Auntie Jill into going."

"What about you?" I asked. "Are you going with them?"

"No, that's the other thing," Fliss said gloomily. "Me and Callum are supposed to go to Dad's for the afternoon."

"Ask your mum if you can come round here

Sleepover Girls on the Ball

instead," I said, thinking fast. "The others'll be here soon, and we can decide what to do."

"OK," Fliss said glumly, and put the phone down.

"Problems?" said my mum. She was standing right behind me.

"No," I said innocently. "We're all going on a bike ride this afternoon, like I told you before."

"That's all right then," said my mum. "Because I know you wouldn't lie to me, Frankie."

"No," I said. Well, it wasn't lying, was it? We *were* going on a bike ride – to the tennis club!

I finished my sandwich and toffee yoghurt in double-quick time, and then went out into the front garden to wait for the others. A few minutes later, Rosie came cycling down the street, followed closely by Kenny.

"We've got a problem, guys," I said, as they wheeled their bikes into the garden. "Fliss's mum and her Auntie Jill have decided to go to the gala afternoon."

Kenny's face fell. "Oh, rats!" she exclaimed.

"Well, we can't go then, can we?" Rosie asked. "If they spot us, we'll be deader than dead!"

The Sleepover Club

"Hey, we can't give up now," Kenny said. "There's going to be loads of people there. I bet we can keep out of their way."

Fliss and Lyndz came pedalling like mad things down the road.

"What're we going to do?" Fliss gasped, jumping off her bike and nearly tripping herself up.

"We'll have to go," Kenny said. "Otherwise the M&Ms are going to start talking to Mrs Morgan, and then they'll find out everything that happened."

"But what about my mum?" Fliss looked as if she was about to faint with fright.

"Look, like I said before, we'll just find the M&Ms, prove that we're there and then leg it," Kenny said. "Come on, let's go."

"Has everyone got their membership cards?" I asked, as we climbed on to our bikes. Everyone nodded, and we cycled off.

When we got to the tennis club we had to hide behind the trees at the side of the road, while we checked the car park to make sure Fliss's mum wasn't parking the car. Then we had to dash out, lock up our bikes and rush over to the entrance, hoping that Mrs Proudlove and

Sleepover Girls on the Ball

Auntie Jill didn't turn up while we were trying to get in. There was quite a long queue at the turnstile, and we joined the end of it.

We were so worried about Fliss's mum, we'd forgotten to check which man was on the gate. Luckily, it wasn't the man from yesterday – it was the same elderly man who'd been there the first time we came. I hoped he wouldn't remember that two days ago, we'd all been guests and not members!

The man was looking a bit stressed out, probably because there were so many people around.

"Membership cards, please," he snapped.

Kenny went first, and handed her card over, looking pretty confident. The guy hardly looked at it this time. He gave it back to Kenny, then flicked his eyes over mine, Fliss's, Lyndz's and Rosie's without even taking them from us.

"Go through," he said shortly.

I could hardly believe it – we were in! Kenny's plan had worked.

Kenny gave us a big grin, and pushed hard against the turnstile.

"Hey!" she gasped, as it didn't move. "It's not working."

The Sleepover Club

The man was staring suspiciously at Rosie. "Give me your card, please," he said, frowning at her.

Rosie looked pretty scared as she handed it over. The man looked at it, and then glared at us.

"We spell *tennis* with two 'n's here," he said angrily, holding the card up so that we could see it.

Green Lawns Tenis Club was printed in black across the top of Rosie's card.

"You idiot, Rosie," Kenny said crossly under her breath.

"I didn't notice I'd spelt it wrong!" Rosie muttered, turning bright red in the face.

"I'll have the rest of those fake cards, please," the man said sternly, holding out his hand. He collected them all up while the people in the queue behind us watched, goggle-eyed. It was totally embarrassing.

"Now be off with you," the man shouted, "or I'll call Security!"

We slunk off back towards the car park, with everyone in the queue turning round to watch us go.

"Rosie, don't you know how to spell *tennis*?" Fliss groaned.

"Of course I do," Rosie said miserably. "Sorry, guys."

"We'd better get our bikes and go," Lyndz suggested, "before Fliss's mum turns up."

We hurried across the car park, but we had to wait as a white van turned in from the road and drove in front of us. It had *Archers Catering Company* written on the side in blue letters.

"It'll be just my luck to meet my mum while we're cycling back to Cuddington," Fliss grumbled, bending down to unlock her bike. "If she ever knew what we'd been up to, I'd be—"

"Don't unlock your bikes yet," Kenny cut in. "Wait a minute."

"Why?" I asked, surprised.

Kenny didn't answer. She was watching the white van very intently. The driver had got out and gone across to speak to the man operating the turnstile. Now he got back in the van again. Slowly, the big iron gates began to open. They must have been controlled automatically by the man in the hut.

"Come on," Kenny whispered.

We hurried over to the gates. The van drove through, and we dashed into the club after it, just before the gates started to close again.

# The Sleepover Club

"Hey! Come back!"

We could hear the man at the turnstile shouting behind us, but we didn't stop.

"No chance, mate," Kenny grinned, punching the air.

CHAPTER TEN

"What do we do now?" Fliss asked, panicking as usual.

"Lose ourselves in the crowd, just in case that guy comes after us," Kenny instructed.

There were loads of people around, and once we'd moved away from the entrance, we felt reasonably safe. The place was packed. By the look of it, there were matches going on on all the courts, and there were lots of people sitting watching them. The restaurant and the clubhouse were full of people eating and drinking and having a good time. There were also a couple of big, white marquees set up on the grass, and people were standing around in the sunshine eating bowls of strawberries and cream. There was bunting in the trees, and stalls selling tennis stuff.

"Right, let's find the M&Ms," Kenny said, looking around.

"It's not going to be easy with all these people," Fliss said. Then she gave a shriek, and grabbed my arm.

"I thought we weren't going to draw attention to ourselves," I reminded her.

"Over there – it's Mark!" Fliss stammered, "He mustn't see us, or he'll tell Auntie Jill."

Mark was standing chatting to another man by the fountain.

"Let's get out of here," Kenny said urgently. She spun round, and knocked a bowl of strawberries and cream right out of the hand of the woman standing behind her.

"Well, really!" said the woman, who was another snooty type in a straw hat and a posh flowery frock.

"Sorry." Kenny scooped the strawberries up, dropped them into the bowl and handed them back to the disgusted woman. "Come on, let's hide!'"

We ran off round the side of the clubhouse,

out of sight. Then we peered round the building to see if Mark had noticed us. He hadn't. He was still chatting to the same guy.

"That was close," Rosie whispered.

"Quick, let's find the M&Ms and get out of here," Fliss pleaded.

Cautiously we came out from behind the clubhouse. But we hadn't gone more than a few steps when we suddenly saw Mrs Proudlove and Auntie Jill, making their way towards us.

"It's my mum," Fliss gasped. As if we didn't know that already!

"Look, follow me," Kenny said quickly, leading us towards one of the marquees. We crept round the side of it, and stood there, our hearts pounding. Well, mine was, and I'm sure everyone else's was too!

"It's OK," said Kenny, who was keeping watch. "They've joined Mark, and now they're all going into the restaurant."

"That'll keep them out of the way for a bit," Fliss said, relieved.

"Let's go to the courts," Rosie suggested. "The M&Ms could be watching one of the matches."

"Good idea, Rosie-Posie," I said. "Come on, then."

Fliss was staring at the flowerbed nearest the marquee. "Hang on," she said, pointing at a plant with big scarlet flowers. "What's that?"

"Fliss, this is no time for gardening questions!" Kenny hissed crossly. "We need to find the M&Ms and get out of here."

"Not the plant, you idiot," Fliss retorted. "That little blue box lying underneath it."

She bent down and picked the box up. It was made of dark blue leather, and had *Masterson's* printed in gold on the top.

"It looks like a jewellery box," Fliss said eagerly. "I wonder if there's anything inside it?"

She was just about to open it, when we heard two angry voices in front of the tent, only a metre or so from where we were standing.

"And first of all they tried to fool me with fake cards, and then they ran inside when the catering van came in!"

We all looked at each other in horror. It was the man from the gate.

"Yes, Mr Harper, you've already told me, several times." I glanced at the others. I recognised that voice. Last time we'd heard it, she'd been telling us off for breaking her precious racket. Mrs Morgan! "And from your description, it sounds like those terrible girls who were responsible for ruining my Aunt Fiona's racket."

Kenny pulled a face. "She's on to us!" she whispered.

"Shall I make an announcement over the tannoy, Mrs Morgan?" Mr Harper went on. "I could put out a description, and ask people to keep an eye open for them."

I rolled my eyes at the others. Honestly, this guy was acting like something out of *The Bill*! It wasn't like we were criminals or anything.

"No, I don't think that's a good idea," Mrs Morgan said. "But, as we both know what they look like, we'd better search for them ourselves."

We didn't dare look to see which direction they were going in. If one of them came round the side of the marquee, we were as good as dead!

"Quick!" Kenny gasped. "Under here!"

She lifted up the canvas, and we all crawled underneath it and into the marquee as fast as we could. Fliss was trying to shove the little blue box in her pocket, and kept dropping it, which held us up a bit.

The marquee was the place where they were serving the strawberries and cream, and what looked like champagne in crystal glasses. It was packed with people, and it could have been a bit embarrassing if we'd been spotted. But luckily, there were lots of long tables, covered with white cloths dotted about, and one of these happened to be positioned right where we'd crept under the canvas. So we were able to slide under the table without anyone seeing us. The tablecloth hung almost right down to the ground, so we were pretty well hidden. We could just see people's shoes moving about.

"What now?" Fliss whispered.

"We'll stay here for a bit, and wait until Mrs Morgan and Mr Harper have gone off somewhere else," Kenny said.

"I'm getting cramp in my legs," I grumbled. The tables were pretty low, and I was so hunched up, I was starting to ache all over. It was all right for the others, they weren't as tall as me.

Sleepover Girls on the Ball

"Stop moving around, Frankie," Rosie said in a panicky voice. "You're rocking the table."

I groaned, trying to stretch my aching arms and legs a bit. "I'm never going to be able to stand up straight again!"

"Hey, what's that?" Kenny jumped as something fell on to the grass, right next to her foot. She peered at it, then grinned at us. "It's OK, guys," she whispered. "Someone's just dropped a spoon."

It took us about two seconds to realise that if somebody had *dropped* a spoon, they'd probably be bending down to pick it up. But it was too late. Someone had already pulled the tablecloth aside, searching for the spoon...

We all looked into the startled face of a woman in a straw hat and a flowery frock. The same woman whose strawberries Kenny had sent flying a little while ago!

"Aargh!" the woman shrieked, jumping backwards. I didn't think we were *that* scary-looking, but I don't suppose she was expecting to see anyone under the table, let alone five of us.

"Quick, let's get out of here!" I gasped. We yanked up the edge of the marquee, and wriggled our way out. Then we jumped to our feet, and dashed off. A few minutes later, we were in the middle of a large crowd, and feeling a lot safer.

"Where are we?" Kenny asked, looking around.

"Near the changing-rooms." I pointed them out. "And there are the courts."

"If we walk along the fence, we can check out the people watching, and see if the M&Ms are there," Lyndz suggested.

"Good idea," I began. But then I nearly *died* as a hand grabbed my shoulder from behind.

"What do you girls think you're doing?" said a stern voice.

We all turned as white as ghosts. But when we looked round, it wasn't Mrs Morgan standing there. It was a shorter, thinner woman wearing glasses and carrying a clipboard.

"N-nothing," I stammered. "We're not doing anything."

"Exactly!" the woman said crossly, rolling her eyes. "What are you hanging around here for? Haven't you been told what to do?"

I glanced at the others. We didn't have a clue what this woman was going on about, but at least she didn't seem to know that we were being hunted by Mrs Morgan.

"Er – no," I said, trying to look as if I knew what she meant. "Not exactly."

The woman tutted loudly. "Come with me," she snapped. "We don't have much time."

She bustled over to the changing-rooms, taking us with her.

"Go and get changed," she said impatiently. "And hurry up about it. I'll wait for you here."

"What?" I stared at her. Get changed? Into what?

"Your uniforms are in the junior changing-rooms," the woman said. "Now get a move on. We haven't got all day."

Feeling a bit dazed, we all trailed into the changing-rooms.

"We need to get away from that mad woman!" Kenny said urgently. "Is there another way out of here?"

I stopped by a door labelled:

JUNIOR CHANGING-ROOM – GIRLS

"Let's look in here. There might be a window we can climb out of or something."

The Sleepover Club

We went in.

"Look." Fliss pointed at five pairs of dark green shorts and five green sports shirts, hanging on pegs near the door.

"Are those our uniforms?" Lyndz asked, puzzled. "What are we supposed to be?"

"She thinks we're ballgirls," Fliss gasped.

"Pardon?" Rosie said.

"Ballgirls," Fliss repeated. "You know, ballboys and ballgirls run around the courts and collect the spare tennis balls during a match."

"What!" Lyndz squeaked anxiously. "I wouldn't have a clue what to do!"

"We've got to get out of here," Kenny said urgently. She went over to the window, climbed on to the bench and tried to open it. "Oh, rats, it's locked."

"What are we going to *do*?" Rosie wailed. "She's waiting for us outside."

"We'll just have to go and tell her we're *not* the ballgirls," I said.

"I'll do it," Kenny offered. She went over to the door, walked out and then leapt back in again. "She's talking to Mrs Morgan!" she hissed.

Sleepover Girls on the Ball

We all nearly *died*.

"Mrs Morgan's probably telling her all about us," Fliss whispered.

"It's OK," Rosie pointed out. "She thinks we're the ballgirls."

"We'll have to go along with it for the moment, until we can leg it," Kenny said. "Come on, get changed."

We all started taking our clothes off, and putting the ballgirls' uniforms on. We had to do a bit of swapping around to make them fit, and even then mine was too tight, and Rosie's shorts were too long.

"It's OK, Mrs Morgan's gone," Kenny said, peering round the door. "Come on."

"Are we *really* going to have to be ballgirls?" Lyndz asked.

"'Course not," Kenny replied. "We'll try and get away as soon as we can."

But it wasn't as easy as that. The woman was still waiting for us outside, and she herded us over to the courts. One of them, Court 3, was absolutely packed with people waiting for a match to start, and as we got closer, we heard the umpire talking to the audience.

The Sleepover Club

"Ladies and gentlemen, thank you for coming to our gala afternoon. Today we have a very special match for you. The winner of the women's club championship last year, Barbara Browne, will be playing the winner from the previous year, Marina Warner."

There was loud applause.

The woman with the clipboard stopped right by Court 3. "Go on, then," she said, pushing the door open. "They're ready to start."

"What, *here*?" Kenny gasped, shooting the rest of us a panicky look. "But there's about ten million people watching!"

"So?" The woman looked at us suspiciously. "You know what to do, don't you? You *are* ballgirls. Aren't you?"

CHAPTER ELEVEN

We were all too nervous to say anything, except Fliss. For once, she didn't panic.

"Of course we are," she said coolly.

"Good." The woman glanced at her clipboard. "Don't forget that one of you has to be in charge of the scoreboard."

Fliss nodded. "Come on, girls," she said confidently, pushing the door open.

We trailed on to the court behind her, trying to make ourselves look as small as possible. The umpire was introducing the players to the audience, so no one was taking much notice of us.

"Look," Fliss said urgently. "You know how to

be ballgirls, don't you?"

We all shook our heads.

"You've seen Wimbledon, haven't you?" Fliss asked, beginning to look desperate.

We shook our heads again.

"OK, listen to me," Fliss went on. "Two of us have to be at the end of the net, one on each side of it, to collect the balls that don't go over."

"Frankie and me can do that," Kenny volunteered.

Fliss nodded. "Then there has to be one person at each end to pass the balls for the players to serve."

"That sounds easy," Rosie said hopefully. "Maybe me and Lyndz can do that."

"All right," Fliss agreed. "But remember, you have to do it like this." She raised one hand high in the air, and pretended to bounce an imaginary ball towards a player. "And I'll do the scoreboard," she went on.

The scoreboard was in the corner, and was just a black board, with white numbers on it, a bit like a cricket scoreboard. It wasn't an automatic one, so the numbers had to be changed by hand. Fliss went over there, and Lyndz and Rosie each went to different ends of

Sleepover Girls on the Ball

the court. They both looked terrified. Meanwhile Kenny and I went over to the net, and hung about. The two players were busy unpacking their sports bags, and having a drink before the match began.

I nudged Kenny. "Fliss is trying to tell us something," I said.

Fliss was pulling faces and pointing at us.

"What's she going on about?" Kenny wanted to know.

Fliss was pointing at her knees, and bending up and down.

"Oh, I get it," I said. Even though I used to hate tennis, I'd seen bits of Wimbledon when my mum was watching it. "She's telling us to remember to crouch down when the match starts."

The players were coming on to the court now, ready to warm up. Marina Warner went down the end where Rosie was standing, and Barbara Brown took the other end. They started knocking the ball around to each other, and practising their serves.

"Hey, Frankie, look," Kenny whispered suddenly. "It's the M&Ms!"

She pointed at the crowd. The M&Ms were

The Sleepover Club

sitting in the middle of a row near the front. They were staring at me and Kenny, their faces absolutely crimson with fury.

"They're really annoyed," Kenny said gleefully. "Wave at them, Frankie."

We flapped our hands at the M&Ms, and they stared back at us, stony-faced. We'd obviously *really* wound them up. I bet they never *dreamt* we'd turn up at the club as ballgirls. Then again, neither did we!

"Do you mind!" Marina Warner came over, glaring at us. "Stop distracting me. And aren't you supposed to be picking these balls up?"

With a bad-tempered look on her face, she pointed her racket at a ball lying by the net. We'd been so busy waving at the M&Ms, we hadn't noticed that there was a ball waiting to be collected.

"OK, don't get your knickers in a twist," Kenny retorted, and she strolled on to the court and picked the ball up.

"I think we're supposed to do it a bit quicker than that!" I told her.

"What do I do now?" Kenny said, staring at the ball in her hand. "Shall I put it in my pocket or what?"

Sleepover Girls on the Ball

Fliss was jumping up and down by the scoreboard, trying to attract our attention as the umpire announced that the game was about to start. I squinted at her.

"I think she's saying you roll it down the court to Lyndz," I told Kenny.

"OK." Kenny shrugged, and rolled the ball down to one end of the court. Unfortunately, Lyndz wasn't looking.

"Lyndz!" Kenny hissed. "*Lyndz!*"

Lyndz jumped, looked down at her feet and saw the ball lying there. At last she picked it up.

"Miss Browne to serve," said the umpire.

The whole court went quiet. Barbara Browne, who looked a whole lot nicer than grumpy Marina Fleming, turned to Lyndz, waiting for a ball to be passed to her so she could serve. Lyndz just smiled at her.

"Lyndz!" I groaned under my breath. "Give her a ball, or the match can't start."

"Oops!" Lyndz said suddenly, turning pink, as she remembered what she was supposed to do. "Sorry." But instead of bouncing the ball to the player like Fliss had shown her, she dashed over and handed it to Barbara Browne. There was a ripple of laughter round the court.

The Sleepover Club

"Quiet, please," said the umpire sharply.

"We've got to do better than this, or we're going to look like real idiots," Kenny fretted. "And won't the M&Ms just love that."

We started concentrating then. It was actually pretty easy, once we got the hang of it. All Kenny and I had to do was dash on to the court and pick up any balls which hit the net, and then roll them down to Rosie or Lyndz, depending on which player was serving. And once Lyndz realised that she was supposed to *bounce* the ball to the player and not *hand* it to them, things went really well.

The only problem was that Marina Warner was a bit bad-tempered. She wasn't such a good player as Barbara Browne, and she got annoyed every time she lost a point.

"She's a miserable so-and-so, isn't she?" Kenny remarked to me, as Marina Warner stomped back to the baseline after hitting the ball into the net.

"Ssh," I said, as Marina shot us a poisonous glare.

Her next serve was in, and Barbara Browne returned it. Marina hit the ball with a forehand drive, and it fell just over the net, near to where Kenny was crouched, but about a centimetre outside the white line.

"Out," called the umpire.

"That was definitely in," Marina snapped, rushing over to him.

"No, it wasn't," Kenny said helpfully. "It *was* out. I saw it."

Marina Warner turned purple. She was so angry, I thought she was going to grab Kenny and shake her.

"Since when have the ballgirls been umpires?" she snorted scornfully.

"I've got eyes, haven't I?" Kenny retorted. "And it was out!"

"Quiet!" the umpire said with a frown. "Carry on with the game, please."

"She's a right pain in the bottom, isn't she?" Kenny said, pulling a face at Marina's back. "I hope she loses!"

She did. Barbara Browne won by two sets to love, and when she hit the winning point, everyone started cheering. So did we! The umpire didn't look too impressed at us joining in, but we didn't care.

"I'm tired out," Kenny moaned, as we joined up with the others. There was a fifteen-minute interval before the next match, and most of the audience were leaving. "You don't think we've got to do this for the *next* match, do you?"

"How about if we swap over?" Rosie suggested. "You and Frankie can change with me and Lyndz."

"Hang on a minute," said Lyndz. "Shouldn't we be getting out of here? I mean, we've seen the M&Ms and they've seen us."

The M&Ms were just leaving the court. They were whispering to each other, and shooting us furious looks.

"Yeah, we've well and truly rubbed their noses in it," Kenny said with satisfaction. "I suppose we'd better go."

"We've been pushing our luck," I pointed out. "Mrs Morgan could have walked on to that court and spotted us at any moment."

We hurried over to the door, and went out with the last few spectators.

"Let's get changed, and get out of here," I said urgently.

"Wait." Kenny grabbed my arm, and yanked me back. "There's that woman again, the one with the clipboard."

Sleepover Girls on the Ball

The woman who'd sent us to get changed was standing talking to a group of five girls, a little bit older than us.

"Do you think they're the *real* ballgirls?" Fliss asked nervously.

We crept behind a nearby bush, and listened hard. We could just about hear what they were saying.

"And your mum's car broke down," the woman was saying suspiciously. "That's why you're late."

"That's right," one of the girls replied.

"Hm, that's strange," the woman went on. "Because we've actually got all our ballgirls, and we've got no uniforms left, anyway."

"But we're *supposed* to be ballgirls," the girl said firmly. "Ask my mum, she's a member here."

"There's something funny going on," the woman said, sounding puzzled. "Come with me, and we'll find Mrs Morgan and see what she says."

They all went off. Immediately we dashed out from behind the bush, and into the changing-rooms.

"Hurry up," Kenny urged us.

The Sleepover Club

We didn't need much persuading. We changed out of our clothes in double-quick time, and then ran for the door. We peered outside to check that the coast was clear, and then we hurried outside.

"Keep a look-out for my mum," Fliss told us, as we headed for the exit.

We nearly made it safely out of the tennis club, too. We wouldn't have stopped if we hadn't seen the M&Ms standing by the fountain...

"Oh, there you are!" the Queen said. Funnily enough, she didn't look annoyed any more. She looked like a cat who'd just had a big saucerful of cream. "We were looking for you."

"Where are you going?" the Goblin chimed in.

"Home," Kenny said breezily. "We've finished being ballgirls. You *did* see us, didn't you?"

"Oh, yes." The Queen folded her arms, looking smug. "But are you *sure* that's what you were meant to be doing?"

She couldn't be on to us – could she?

"What are you talking about?" I asked.

"We heard Mrs Morgan talking to somebody, and she said five girls had got into the club,

Sleepover Girls on the Ball

who weren't members," Emma Hughes said gleefully. "It was *you*, wasn't it?"

We all tried not to look guilty.

"Don't be stupid," Kenny retorted. "How could we have been ballgirls if we weren't meant to be here?"

"I don't know." The Queen frowned. "But we're going to tell Mrs Morgan right away, aren't we, Emily?"

"Yeah," Emily agreed eagerly.

"I wouldn't do that if I were you!" Kenny growled, taking a sudden step towards them.

Emma Hughes panicked, and jumped backwards. She knocked into the fountain behind her, sat down in surprise for a moment on the edge of it, and then tipped backwards, her legs and arms waving.

"Help!" she shrieked as she fell into about half a metre of not-very-clean water.

We all burst out laughing, except for the Goblin, of course.

"Serves you right," Kenny grinned, walking up to the edge of the fountain. "*Aaargh!*"

We all gasped as Kenny slipped on a patch of water, and went flying. She landed heavily on the ground, and we rushed over to her.

# The Sleepover Club

"Are you OK, Kenny?" Lyndz said anxiously. Kenny's face was white. "No," she said through gritted teeth. "I think… I think I've sprained my ankle!"

CHAPTER TWELVE

"Serves *you* right, Laura McKenzie!" yelled Emily Berryman. She was trying to help Emma out of the fountain. The Queen was dripping wet from head to toe.

"Everyone's looking," Fliss said nervously. People sitting outside on the restaurant patio were staring at us. "Can you walk, Kenny?"

Kenny was trying to pull herself to her feet, hanging on to the edge of the fountain. "I don't know," she gasped, looking as if she was in a lot of pain. "You'll have to help me."

Lyndz and I put our arms round her, and we began to make our way slowly towards the exit, with Kenny leaning on us and hopping along.

The Sleepover Club

We left the Goblin trying to dry the Queen off with her hanky.

"How is Kenny going to cycle home?" Rosie asked suddenly.

We all looked at each other in dismay.

"She isn't," I said at last.

"I can try," Kenny said bravely, putting her injured foot down on the ground for a second. "Ow!"

"So what're we going to do?" Lyndz asked.

"We could find Fliss's mum and tell her what's happened," Rosie suggested. "Then she could give us a lift."

Fliss turned a sickly green colour. "She'd be so mad, I'd be grounded till I'm eighteen," she muttered.

"There must be a phone here," I said. "We could ring one of our parents, and get them to pick us up."

"Then *they'll* want to know what we're doing here," Rosie said gloomily.

None of us could think of anything to say. We seemed to have got ourselves into the worst mess *ever*. It didn't look like there was anything we could do except own up.

"Hello, girls," said a voice behind us.

Sleepover Girls on the Ball

We all nearly jumped out of our skins. We turned round to find Mark standing there. He was frowning, and looked pretty upset.

"H-hello," we gulped, waiting for him to start yelling at us.

But Mark didn't seem too worried about us being there. In fact, he just didn't seem interested at all. He wasn't even looking at us. He was glancing all around him, as if he was looking for someone or something.

"Maybe you could help me, girls," he said urgently. "I've lost something, and it's really important that I find it again. You could help me search for it."

"Sorry," Kenny said. "I've sprained my ankle."

"And we were just leaving," Fliss added quickly.

"What have you lost?" I asked. I felt a bit sorry for Mark, he looked so worried.

"A little blue box," Mark told me, "with gold writing on the top."

"Oh!" Fliss dived into her pocket, and pulled out the box she'd picked up in the flowerbed when we were hiding round the side of the marquee. "I'd forgotten about it,

The Sleepover Club

what with – er – everything going on. Is this it?"

Mark's face lit up as if someone had just given him a million pounds.

"That's it!" he said, looking hugely relieved. "It must have fallen out of the pocket of my shorts. I can't thank you enough, girls." He took the box from Fliss, then frowned. "How did you girls get in here, anyway? You didn't come with Nikky and Jill, did you?"

We'd been rumbled. Should we own up, or try to think of a way out? Kenny was in too much pain to come up with one of her 'brilliant' plans, and to be honest, I couldn't think of anything myself.

"Felicity! What are *you* doing here?"

Too late. Fliss's mum and Auntie Jill had appeared from nowhere, and were charging towards us. Fliss almost fainted on the spot, and the rest of us weren't far behind her.

"I can't believe it!" Mrs Proudlove said, looking dazed. "What on *earth* are you girls doing here?"

"And how did you get in?" Auntie Jill added.

No one got a chance to say anything more though. Suddenly the M&Ms came out of the

Sleepover Girls on the Ball

clubhouse. Emma Hughes had a towel round her shoulders, and she looked triumphant when she saw us.

"There they are, Mrs Morgan!" she shouted.

We were all horrified. Next moment the club secretary rushed out of the clubhouse behind the M&Ms, and glared at us.

"Aha!" she said loudly. "So there you are. You've led me a merry dance, haven't you?"

She stomped down the clubhouse steps, and rushed over to us. The M&Ms followed her, grinning.

"Oh, dear," Fliss's mum said nervously. "I hope these girls haven't been a nuisance again, Mrs Morgan."

"Worse than that." The club secretary folded her arms grimly. "I have reason to believe that they forced their way into this club without proper membership cards."

We all hung our heads and looked sheepish. We were really in for it now. And didn't the M&Ms just love it. They were both lapping it up.

"Actually that's not true, Mrs Morgan," Mark said suddenly.

What?

The Sleepover Club

"The girls are here as my guests," Mark went on. Mrs Morgan and the M&Ms looked really taken aback, and Fliss's mum and Auntie Jill stared at him.

"*Your* guests?" Mrs Morgan repeated fiercely.

Mark nodded. "You see," he went on, "this is a very special occasion."

Suddenly, for some reason, he got down on one knee. We all goggled at him.

"What's he up to?" Kenny whispered. "Has he gone barmy?"

Mark took Auntie Jill's hand, and then flipped the box open. We saw the sparkle of a diamond inside.

"Jill, please will you marry me?" he said.

CHAPTER THIRTEEN

Everyone was *stunned*. There was silence for a few seconds, and then Auntie Jill burst into tears.

"Just say YES!" Kenny whispered.

"Yes, Mark," Auntie Jill sobbed happily, as he slid the ring on to her finger. "Of course I'll marry you!"

We all began to cheer. Fliss was nearly wetting herself with excitement, Mrs Proudlove was crying too and hugging her sister and Mark, and the people in the restaurant stood up and started clapping. Even Mrs Morgan looked pleased. Only the M&Ms slunk off, still looking grumpy!

"This is great!" Lyndz grinned.

"Yeah, maybe I'll get to be a bridesmaid," Fliss said excitedly.

Mark came over to us. "Thanks, girls," he said, with a wink. "If it hadn't been for you, I might never have got that ring back. And I'd been saving up for it for weeks."

"Thank *you* for saving our necks," Kenny whispered.

Mark smiled at us. "No problem. Especially as Fliss and I are going to be related now."

Fliss turned pink. "Yeah, you'll be my uncle," she said.

Mrs Proudlove and Auntie Jill came over to us, and we all crowded round to look at the engagement ring.

"Mrs Morgan has very kindly offered us glasses of champagne to celebrate," Fliss's mum told Mark.

"Great!" Kenny said.

"It's orange juice for you, girls," Mrs Proudlove said with a smile. "And Kenny, I think we'd better get you to the first-aid tent, so that they can take a look at your ankle."

Half an hour later, we were all sitting out on the patio in the sunshine. We had orange juice,

Sleepover Girls on the Ball

and big bowls of delicious strawberries and cream, and we scoffed the lot! Kenny's ankle had been looked at, and she was resting her leg on a chair. The guy in the first-aid tent had given her an ice-pack, and told her that it was a bad sprain, and not to walk on it if she could help it.

"You know, maybe we should join the tennis club ourselves," Kenny said, finishing off her strawberries. "I reckon we could become members, if Mark put in a good word for us."

"Hm, we'll have to see about that," said Fliss's mum.

"Hang on a minute, Kenny." Fliss suddenly put down her spoon. "Now that you've sprained your ankle, you won't be able to pay in the tennis tournament on Friday."

Kenny's face fell. "Oh, rats!" she said. "And I was looking forward to thrashing the M&Ms. Today's only Wednesday, though," she went on hopefully. "Maybe I'll be OK by Friday."

"No, you won't be," said Mrs Proudlove firmly.

Kenny turned to me. "It's up to you, then, Frankie," she said. "You'll have to take my place."

"But I'm not as good as you," I said, feeling a bit scared, even though I really did want to play.

"Don't put yourself down, Frankie," Mark cut in. "You've got the makings of a killer serve, and your ground shots aren't bad either, for a beginner."

"Thanks," I mumbled, turning red. "OK, I'll play then."

The others cheered. Fliss leaned across the table and clinked glasses with me.

"We're going to beat the pants off the M&Ms," she said. "Just you wait and see."

"And don't forget that there's a sleepover at my place on Friday evening," Lyndz added.

"We'll be celebrating!" Fliss boasted confidently.

"You bet," I said, trying not to sound too nervous...

"I'm really nervous," I said to Fliss, for about the millionth time.

It was the last day of our week of coaching, and the day of the tournament. We were hanging around, waiting for Mark to tell us who we would be playing.

Sleepover Girls on the Ball

Most of our parents had come along to watch, and they were sitting on folding chairs which had been placed around the courts. Rosie's mum was there, my mum had come with Izzy, and Lyndz's mum had come with her baby brother Spike. Kenny had arrived on crutches her dad had given her (he's a doctor, remember?) with Mrs McKenzie, and Mrs Proudlove and Auntie Jill were there too. They were going to help with the umpiring, and so were some of the other parents.

The M&Ms were all dressed up in their gruesome tennis whites and looking completely smug, which annoyed me. They kept well away from us, though, after what had happened at the club!

Mark came over carrying a clipboard.

"Morning, everyone," he called. "Now, let me explain what's going to happen. We've got eight pairs of players, so there'll be four matches to start off with. We're going to draw names out of a bag to see who plays first."

Mark had a box with folded-up bits of paper in it, and Auntie Jill came over and drew them out one by one. Rosie and Lyndz got Ryan and Danny in the first round, and me

The Sleepover Club

and Fliss got Seema and Zoë, who we didn't know very well.

"I don't think they're very good though," Fliss said to me in a low voice.

The M&Ms got Jack and Katie Marshall. They were twins, and they were quite good players, but, of course, the M&Ms were so sure they were going to win, they didn't even look worried.

"Wouldn't it be great if they got knocked out in the first round?" I said to Fliss, as we went over to our court. Rosie and Lyndz were playing Ryan and Danny on the court next to us, so that Kenny could watch both matches at the same time. One of the other parents was umpiring our match, and Fliss's mum was in charge of Rosie and Lyndz's. Each match was only going to be one set long, to save time.

"Come on, Sleepover Club!" Kenny bawled, waving her crutches in the air as we took our places on the court.

"I hope I can remember what to do," I said, feeling worried, as I got ready to serve. Seema and Zoë were already standing on the other side of the net.

"You'll be fine," Fliss said. "I'll remind you if you get things wrong."

Sleepover Girls on the Ball

Rosie and Lyndz were waiting to start their match, but Ryan and Danny were arguing about which one of them was going to serve first. Fliss's mum went over to sort them out. Meanwhile, we waved at Rosie and Lyndz, and yelled, "Good luck!"

I was really nervous, as I tried to remind myself of all the things Mark had told us. I threw the ball up into the air, and hit it. It bounced on the other side of the net, and zoomed past Seema. It was an ace!

"Fifteen-love," called the umpire.

After that, I started to relax a bit. I wasn't really very good, whatever Mark said (after all, I'd only been playing for a week!) but Seema and Zoë were worse than I was! They gave loads of points away because they kept hitting the ball out of the court. Anyway, Fliss was brilliant, and she won most of our points, although I did manage another couple of aces. By the end of the set, the score was six games to two, to me and Fliss. We'd won!

"Brilliant!" Kenny yelled, hobbling around on her crutches and getting a telling-off from her mum.

The Sleepover Club

About ten minutes before our match ended, Rosie and Lyndz finished thrashing the pants off Ryan and Danny. They'd beaten them 6-0. Not surprising really, considering that Ryan and Danny spent the whole time arguing!

"Great stuff," Kenny said, beaming all over her face when we went to speak to her.

"Looks like the M&Ms won as well though," I said.

We looked at the M&Ms, who were strolling back from their court. They were so cocky, it was sickening.

"Well done, all the winners," Mark called, "and bad luck to the losers. Now, I need the four winning teams over here, and we'll draw the names again for the semi-finals."

Mark asked one of the other parents to do the draw this time. The four winning pairs were me and Fliss, Rosie and Lyndz, the M&Ms and two girls called Tania and Natalie. We'd already worked out that either me and Fliss or Rosie and Lyndz could be playing the M&Ms. If we weren't, we would be playing against each other. I didn't know which was worse.

Sleepover Girls on the Ball

"Right, our first semi-final is between Natalie and Tania," Mark called out, "and Fliss and Frankie."

"That means Rosie and Lyndz have got the M&Ms," I groaned to Fliss.

Rosie and Lyndz both looked glum. Meanwhile, the Queen and the Goblin could hardly stop themselves laughing.

"We're going to walk it!" I heard Emma Hughes crowing.

Poor old Rosie and Lyndz looked really down as they trailed over to the court behind the M&Ms.

"Good luck," Fliss and I said together.

Rosie and Lyndz were too depressed even to reply. They just nodded miserably.

"Oh no!" Kenny gasped, when Fliss and I went to tell her who we were playing. "Do you think Rosie and Lyndz will beat the M&Ms?"

"I don't know," I said doubtfully. "Emma Hughes is good."

"You and Fliss could be playing the M&Ms in the final," Kenny pointed out.

"We've got to win first," Fliss said. "And Natalie's pretty good too."

The M&Ms were already knocking up on the court next to ours. Instead of hitting the ball straight back to Rosie and Lyndz, so that they could practise their shots too, they were showing off by belting it out of their reach. Rosie and Lyndz were looking gloomier and gloomier.

Meanwhile, me and Fliss started our game against Tania and Natalie. For the first few minutes, I kept squinting at the next courts, trying to see what was going on between Rosie and Lyndz and the M&Ms. But then I had to start concentrating on *our* game. Natalie was nearly as good as Fliss, and me and Tania were about the same, so it was a really close match.

"That's four games all," Mrs Scott, Ryan's mum called, as Fliss did this really excellent, cross-court backhand to win us the fourth game.

"Try to hit the ball towards Tania, if you can, Frankie," Fliss whispered to me, as Natalie got ready to serve. "She's not very good."

"About as hopeless as me, you mean!" I said. Natalie's serves were quite powerful, and I'd hardly managed to return one of them yet. If it wasn't for Fliss, we'd be losing.

Sleepover Girls on the Ball

I waited for Natalie to serve to me again. This time, for some reason, it wasn't as hard as the others had been. I returned it with a forehand which sent the ball flashing right past Tania, who just stood and looked at it helplessly. It was a fluke, but we'd won the point!

"Love-fifteen," Mrs Scott called.

"Well done, Frankie!" Fliss said, looking thrilled.

Natalie served to Fliss next, and Fliss won the point with a scorching backhand that just skimmed the top of the net. Love-thirty. I lost the next point when Natalie served an ace, which made it fifteen-thirty, but then Fliss won the next. Thirty-forty. We needed one point to win the game, and then one more game to win the set.

"Come on, Frankie," I muttered, as Natalie prepared to serve to me again. "Concentrate."

The ball bounced over the net towards me – and I completely mis-hit it! But it didn't matter. The ball fell gently back over the net, and although Tania made a run forwards, it was too late.

Well, after we'd won that game, there was no stopping me and Fliss. She served for the match, and we won the last game in about two minutes. I think Tania and Natalie had given up by then!

"We're in the final!" Fliss crowed, slapping me on the shoulder.

I suddenly remembered the other match. "Yeah, but who are we playing?" I asked.

We both looked over at the next court. Rosie and Lyndz were walking off, looking depressed, and the M&Ms were laughing and doing high fives.

"It looks like poor old Rosie and Lyndz lost," Fliss said sadly.

"So that means you and me are playing the M&Ms," I groaned.

CHAPTER FOURTEEN

I was so nervous, and it was so quiet, I thought that everyone watching would be able to hear my heart thumping away. I tried to stop my knees wobbling, and looked across the court at Emma Hughes. She was getting ready to serve to me, and she was taking *ages*, bouncing the ball and pulling her skirt down and fiddling with her racket.

"Emma, get on with it, please," called Mark, who was umpiring the match.

Kenny had warned us that the Queen would try to distract us. She'd done the same in the match against Rosie and Lyndz. *And* she'd kept arguing that balls were in or out when they're weren't. Well, Fliss and I were ready for her…

Er – well, maybe we weren't. Emma's serve came zooming towards me, and I hit it weakly into the net. First point to the M&Ms. I heard Kenny groan from the side of the court.

The M&Ms won the first game without me and Fliss winning a single point, which was a bit worrying. As we swapped ends, I was beginning to feel more and more nervous. Fliss would have had a much better chance if she was playing with Kenny, I kept telling myself, and that made me feel even worse.

And now it was my turn to serve. I felt sick.

"Just take it slowly, Frankie," Fliss said. "Remember the things Mark told us."

I nodded. But that was easier said than done. My first serve didn't even get over the net. Neither did my second.

"Love-fifteen," Mark called.

My serving was *hopeless*. I just about managed to get the rest of them in, but they were so slow and pathetic, the M&Ms were banging the ball back all over the place. It was only because Fliss was so brilliant, and Emily

Sleepover Girls on the Ball

Berryman not very good, that we actually won the game. Now it was 1-1.

I cheered up a bit when Emily Berryman had to serve. She was pretty rubbish. Her first serve was just over the line, and Mark called "Out."

"I thought that was in," the Queen said, glaring at him.

Mark shook his head. "Play on, please," he said. He obviously wasn't going to let the Queen get away with wasting time.

Emma looked furious, but she shut up. Anyway, the M&Ms won that game, and the score was 2-1.

It was Fliss's turn to serve, to the Goblin. It was a really good one too, but Berryman just about managed to hit it back over the net. It came towards me, pretty slowly – I pulled back my racket, whacked it and it sailed right out of the court.

I felt *terrible*. And the M&Ms' nasty grins weren't helping. Luckily, Fliss just about managed to turn the game by serving two aces in a row, and then the Goblin fluffed an easy shot, and hit it into the net. So now it was two games each.

That was how it went on for a bit. 3-2. 3-3. 4-3. 4-4. I was so wrapped up in the game, I even forgot about the audience, although I could hear Kenny, Lyndz and Rosie cheering every time we won a point. But if it wasn't for Fliss, we'd have been losing really badly.

The M&Ms had just won the last game, and the score was 5-4. They only had to win one more game, and they'd won the match. As we swapped ends, the Queen smirked at Fliss and me.

"You losers haven't got a hope," she said gleefully. "It's Frankie's turn to serve, and she's useless!"

"Yeah, bye-bye, losers," the Goblin added.

I clutched my tennis racket angrily. That had *really* wound me up.

"Don't get mad, Frankie," Fliss whispered, as the game began again, "Get even!"

"I will," I promised grimly.

The Queen was faffing around on the other side of the net, trying to put me off. I took no notice. I threw the ball into the air, and hit it. It was so fast, the M&Ms didn't even *see* it.

"Fifteen-love," Mark called.

Sleepover Girls on the Ball

I served again. This time Emma Hughes hit it back, straight into the net. Love-thirty.

The M&Ms were starting to look rattled, and that cheered me up no end. I fired down another ace! Love-forty.

The last point of the game was quite a long rally, and Fliss won it with a brilliant backhand. The score was now 5-5.

Emma Hughes was beginning to look really worried. It was the Goblin's turn to serve, and we all knew she wasn't very good. I gritted my teeth, telling myself to concentrate. Fliss and I now had a chance to win this match!

The Goblin was so nervous, she began by serving a double fault. Love-fifteen. The Queen started telling her off, and that made Emily even more nervous. She hit this pathetic, weedy serve that just about made it over the net, and I hit it back, a bit too hard. Luckily, it just stayed inside the white lines, and Emma returned it, in Fliss's direction. Fliss sent it whizzing back, straight between the M&Ms, who both stuck their rackets out and missed.

The score was now love-thirty, and Kenny and the others were going mad at the side of the court. Two more points, and we'd won the match!

The Goblin did us a real favour then, by serving another double fault. The Queen was so furious, I thought she was going to bash Emily over the head with her tennis racket!

"One more point, and we've done it, Frankie," Fliss whispered.

Emily was serving to me now, and pulling all these faces to put me off. I ignored her, and kept my eyes on the ball. It came over the net towards me, I stepped forward, I hit it – and what a shot, even though I say so myself! It zoomed across the court in front of the M&Ms, bounced neatly in the corner and rolled out of play. We'd done it!

"Frankie!" Fliss squealed, flinging her arms around me. "We won! We won!"

I just about had time to catch a glimpse of the M&Ms, red in the face and stomping off the court, when Rosie and Lyndz came dashing over to grab me and hug me too. Kenny couldn't run, obviously, but she was waving one of her crutches in the air like a mad thing.

"You were great, Frankie," she shouted.

Sleepover Girls on the Ball

"Thanks," I yelled back. "Wimbledon, here I come!"

"Show us your winning forehand again, Frankie," Kenny said, with a big grin.

"OK." I got up from the grass, and picked up my new racket. "I kind of stepped forward like *this*, and hit the ball like *this*."

Everyone clapped. It was Friday evening, and we were round at Lyndz's house. We were having our tennis sleepover, and to start with, we'd been having a sort of game in the back garden. It wasn't a proper court, of course, but it was good fun. Kenny had been umpire, and had made up all sorts of stupid rules, like we lost a point if a ball hit a tree, or if it bounced on the path. Or if Buster, Lyndz's mad dog, ran off with the ball!

"I can't believe I've got my own racket," I said proudly. The prize for the winners of the tournament had been a new racket each, and Fliss and I were showing them off. Fliss had brought her old racket, too, for Rosie and Lyndz to share. After playing a game for a while, we'd had some daft competitions, made up by Kenny. One of them was seeing how long you could bounce a tennis ball on your racket for, and another was trying to balance the end of your racket on your finger!

"I'm going to ask for a racket for my birthday," Rosie said.

"Me too," Lyndz added.

"And me," Kenny agreed. "Or maybe I could just use my crutches!"

"Stay where you are," I ordered her, as she started to struggle to her feet. "Your mum said you're not to move around."

"Weren't the M&Ms really sick at losing to us?" Fliss said with satisfaction. "I've never *seen* them so mad!"

"I thought the Queen was going to hit someone with her tennis racket!" Rosie said, and we all giggled.

Just then Lyndz's mum called down the garden. "Tea's ready, girls," she said. "I've laid it all out on the patio."

We were all starving, and we charged down the garden. Well, except for Kenny, of course! We couldn't believe what we saw – Mrs Cartwright had really gone to town. She'd tried to make all the food something to do with tennis. There were racket-shaped sandwiches that must have taken her ages to cut out, and round things like Maltesers and cheesy footballs in bowls. There were strawberries and cream, of course, and right in the middle of the table was a big cake, with a tennis court iced on top of it. There were mini-rackets and tennis balls made of marzipan, and across the court was iced Well Done Frankie and Fliss!

"This is brilliant!" Fliss gasped.

We all stuffed ourselves silly, then we went inside to watch some of Fliss's tennis videos, which she'd brought with her. This time we didn't complain at all – we were glued to the screen. Watching the world-class players made you realise just how difficult it was to play tennis properly. Anyway, I was determined to get better, now that I had my new racket!

"Time for bed, girls," said Lyndz's mum, coming into the living room. "Kenny, you'd better go upstairs and use the bathroom first."

"OK." Kenny pulled herself to her feet, and grinned at us. "We really showed the M&Ms, didn't we?"

"Yeah, we did!" we chorused gleefully.

"Let's carry on playing tennis over the summer," Rosie suggested, as Mrs Cartwright helped Kenny upstairs. "When Kenny's ankle's better, we could go to the courts at the park."

"Maybe my mum will take us back to Green Lawns," Fliss said hopefully. "Or maybe Mark will, now that he's going to be my uncle!"

"When's the wedding?" Lyndz asked.

Fliss shrugged. "I don't know," she replied. "But Auntie Jill's asked me to be a bridesmaid."

"Maybe all the bridesmaids should wear tennis dresses!" I joked.

Fliss gave me a look. "I don't think so," she snorted, as we went upstairs. "I want a *proper* bridesmaid's dress, thank you!"

Kenny was already in bed when we went upstairs. Usually we all lie in our sleeping bags on the floor, but Lyndz's mum thought that Kenny would be better in Lyndz's bed, what with her bad ankle. So Lyndz was on the floor with the rest of us.

"I was thinking," Kenny said, as the rest of us came back from the bathroom. "We ought to carry on playing tennis for the rest of the summer, once my ankle's better."

"That's just what we were saying." I replied, chucking my toothbrush into my sleepover bag.

Sleepover Girls on the Ball

"We could have our own tournament at the end of the summer," Kenny suggested, as everyone unzipped their sleeping bags, and crawled in.

"EEK!" Rosie shrieked suddenly. She was the first one to snuggle down into her sleeping bag. "There's something hairy at the bottom!"

"There's something in mine too!" Fliss screamed, wriggling out again.

"And mine!" Lyndz yelped.

I could feel something too. I pulled myself out of my sleeping bag, and turned it upside-down. Three tennis balls fell out.

"Very funny, Kenny!" I said, as the others did the same and more balls bounced out. Meanwhile, Kenny was laughing her head off in the corner!

"Fifteen-love to me!" she said gleefully.

"No way," I said. I picked up the balls and began chucking them at her, and so did the others. Kenny gave a yell, and tried to hide under the duvet. "Fifteen-all, I think!"

Order Form

To order direct from the publishers, just make a list of the titles you want and fill in the form below:

Name ....

Address ....

....

....

Send to: Dept 6, HarperCollins Publishers Ltd, Westerhill Road, Bishopbriggs, Glasgow G64 2QT.

Please enclose a cheque or postal order to the value of the cover price, plus:

UK & BFPO: Add £1.00 for the first book, and 25p per copy for each additional book ordered.

Overseas and Eire: Add £2.95 service charge. Books will be sent by surface mail but quotes for airmail despatch will be given on request.

A 24-hour telephone ordering service is available to holders of Visa, MasterCard, Amex or Switch cards on 0141- 772 2281.

Collins

An imprint of HarperCollinsPublishers